PENGUIN BOOKS

SPLIT

Meenakshi Reddy Madhavan decided she wanted to become an author at sixteen, and didn't change her mind even when she turned thirty-three and was faced with the bleak financial reality of it. Her first book deal came out of her popular blog Compulsive Confessions (www.compulsiveconfessions.com), which she has been running as a passion project for the last eleven years. She is also the author of three other novels: *You Are Here*, *The Life and Times of Layla the Ordinary* and *Cold Feet* as well as a short story collection called *Before, and Then After*. She lives in New Delhi with her partner and their three cats. She hopes to move to Goa soon.

(Say hi! On Twitter [twitter.com/reddymadhavan], photos of cats on Instagram [Instagram.com/decemberschild] and on Facebook [www.facebook.com/thecompulsiveconfessor]. She'd love to hear from you, even if it's just to talk about the weather we're having.)

ALSO BY MEENAKSHI REDDY MADHAVAN

FOR YOUNG ADULTS

The Life and Times of Layla the Ordinary

FOR ADULTS

You Are Here
Cold Feet
Before, and Then After

Split

MEENAKSHI REDDY
MADHAVAN

PENGUIN BOOKS

An imprint of Penguin Random House

PENGUIN BOOKS

USA | Canada | UK | Ireland | Australia
New Zealand | India | South Africa | China | Singapore

Penguin Books is part of the Penguin Random House group of companies
whose addresses can be found at global.penguinrandomhouse.com

Published by Penguin Random House India Pvt. Ltd
4th Floor, Capital Tower 1, MG Road,
Gurugram 122 002, Haryana, India

First published by Penguin Books India 2015

10 9 8 7 6 5 4 3 2

ISBN 9780143425618

Typeset in Dante MT by R. Ajith Kumar, New Delhi

Printed at Repro India Limited

www.penguin.co.in

For my mother, who stayed.

They fuck you up, your mum and dad,
They may not mean to, but they do.

—Philip Larkin

1

Anyone looking at Noor Khan Rai's face would first stop at her pleasing eyes—long-lashed and heavy-lidded, helped along by an artfully applied smudge of kohl when she could get away with it—then maybe move their gaze up to her wide forehead, where her straight ('limp,' Noor would be quick to point out) hair fell in bangs, almost obscuring one set of eyelashes. Maybe then this observer would also clock her mouth, a nice mouth, corners always tilted up, even in repose. ('I *wish* I had resting bitch face. People always think I'm weak.')

They would probably not notice—even though Noor was convinced they would—her slightly lopsided ears, her uneven and thick eyebrows ('Everyone *else's* parents let them get their eybrows threaded!') or the flat bridge of her mostly perky nose ('like a pakoda').

The more insightful viewer might pay attention to the square set of her round jaw, defying gene pools and ancestry to give her a look of wilful stubbornness that was all her own. 'A determined young lady,' they might say to themselves.

But Noor Khan Rai looked like what most people said when they saw her: 'a sweet girl'. No one is a mind reader, which was fortunate for Noor, because then no one could see past the bangs and the forehead, into her brain where she kept all her Deep Dark Thoughts.

Such as: LOVE IS FOR LOSERS.

Such as: I HATE MY MOTHER.

Such as: I WOULD DO ANYTHING TO NOT BE HERE RIGHT NOW.

*

'So, I'm thinking, about fifteen to twenty people *tops*.' Armana glanced around the room to make sure she had everyone's attention. Which went without saying. People sat up and listened when Armana talked.

Noor noticed her gestures though—like the alpha dog in a pack, Armana had to make sure her followers knew who was in charge. One of these was to look around the room, the way she was doing now, and make eye contact with everybody. 'I am superior to you,' the eye contact said, and whomever she was looking at would do the human equivalent of putting her ears back and letting out an ingratiating whine. In this case, it was Sonum, and Sonum tucked her hair behind her ears and grinned nervously at Armana. Satisfied, Armana glanced around the room again. 'Someone should be writing this down,' she said. 'Noor? You're good with guest lists and shit.'

Noor focused again on what Armana was saying. Her group—which was actually the Group, capital G—very well sounded out among people not fortunate enough to be in it—was four other girls she had known for six years. All of them were pretty—pretty enough to be in the group, and yet, not as pretty as Armana, who was the school beauty, all pale skin and wasp waist and just tall enough for people to tell her she should be a model but not so tall that she couldn't find boys to date. They all played their own roles—Natasha was into music, Sanvi was the rebel, Sonum was the rich, fat girl whose house they did all their sleepovers at and Noor was the 'nice' one (mostly). Armana was the pretty one, of course, but even Armana could only date one boy at a time, so she shared the distinction of being a Girlfriend with Sanvi, whose boyfriend Aryan was in first-year college and a secret from her parents. He bought them alcohol and cigarettes.

Noor had once asked Sanvi what she liked about Aryan. 'He's cute, I guess,' Sanvi had shrugged. 'He kisses nicely. And the Mishras would *kill* me if they found out.'

This was before Noor had started going through her family-hating period, and she had found it so strange that Sanvi resented her parents so much. She had their numbers saved as 'Mr Mishra Cell' and 'Mrs Mishra Cell' and, once, when they had called from the landline, Noor had seen the word 'Hell' flash on the phone's caller ID. She had met the Mishras—they were very conservative and insisted Sanvi do all the household chores every weekend, like rolling out rotis with her mother or learning how to tie a sari with her sister-in-law. She mostly wore salwar kameezes at home and smuggled her Western wear to school. She usually bought it online and had it delivered to the house of one of the girls in the Group.

'Helloooo, Noor, where are you?' Armana's sing-song voice cut in. 'I've asked you, like, thirty times. Pay attention, please. Will you do the guest list for my party this week?'

'Yes,' said Noor, and pulled out a glitter pen and her party-planning notebook. Everyone else had an iPad or, at least, a cheap tablet, but 'Screen time is not good for you, Noorie,' said her family, so she was stuck with notebooks. At least they didn't skimp on that. So she bought pretty ones and plain ones and ones with leather covers and ones with watercolour handmade paper. This one was a plain spiral notebook that said, 'I Heart Pugs', a picture of a pug under the heart. Very hipster. Pugs were seeing a general revival at Noor's regular stationary store.

She wrote down all their names as she always did:

Armana
Natasha
Sanvi
Sonum
&
Noor

She always put her name at the bottom of the list. She liked seeing the other girls' names before hers—it was like she was shielded from the world by the force of their names. But now that she thought about it, if someone bumped into all their names, hers would be the first one to drift off, broken away, shattered by impact.

Usually, when she wrote her own name down, she put eyebrows over the Os and a smile underneath, but today she made the eyebrows slant and the mouth turn downwards. There.

Armana had a list in her hand from which she read out names, which Noor wrote down dutifully.

'We'll send an e-vite—Facebook invitations are so tacky, plus, anyone can see them,' Armana said.

The Group liked everyone to know about their parties, so they left the Facebook invitation public, but they didn't like everyone to come. Over the past few gatherings, maintaining exclusivity had been hard, especially since people kept crashing. 'Do an invite-only e-vite,' Armana was saying, 'and then you can post the image on Facebook. Be, like, super mysterious about it, though . . . Don't want randos showing up, like, yuck, those losers from last time.'

The Group had a list of what was considered loser-like behaviour, which was usually a running list of the things Armana disapproved of. Currently, it included:

1. Liking Old Delhi ('So activist-type or something.')
2. Liking GK-1 ('So 2001. What are we, ancient?')
3. Wearing crop tops if you had any fat at all on your stomach ('Ew, no one wants to see that.')
4. Wearing gold instead of silver jewellery ('What are you, a Madrasi aunty?')
5. Boys who wore pants high around their waists ('Um. Preparing for a flood?')
6. Boys who brought tiffin boxes ('Vom.')

7. Girls who brought tiffin boxes ('The smell never leaves your general . . . area. It's like you have this aura of *adrak*. An adraura!')

8. Anyone picking her up in a car that wasn't a 'nice' car ('No. I would rather take an *auto*. I would rather *walk*. I'm not getting in that fucking car.')

9. Eating at any fast-food place that wasn't Subway ('Yeah, that stuff is *poison* and I'm not doing it, and God knows how much rat shit went into that burger.')

'Nuts, you'll do the music, yeah? Just, like, keep it to good music this time. Last time people were complaining there was nothing to dance to.'

Natasha looked glum but she agreed. Noor knew she hated to 'pander to the squalling crowds', as she called it. 'My life is not a Top-40, Noor!' she would rant. 'If I'm ever going to be a great DJ, I need to play stuff that will get people to listen to something new, not the same song over and over again!'

Listening to the pop hits was *not* loser-like behaviour because Armana loved pop hits. However, listening to 'that awful music with no words and this weird "ounce ounce" in the background like some kind of drug fiend' was loser-like behaviour, only forgiven in Natasha because Armana liked her. If Natasha played her music, Armana would shake her head lovingly at her and say, 'You're *so* weird, Nuts.'

Once, at one of their parties, Noor had overheard someone bitch about Natasha's taste in music in front of Armana, and Armana had tipped her head back and looked at them frostily and said, 'It's obvious you guys have no taste. I'm kind of embarrassed *for* you, actually.' The person who made the remark had tried to laugh it off nervously but Armana just kept staring at her until she crumbled and left. Noor remembered the sharp stab of love she had felt for Armana in that moment, for all her *friends*. They were so lovely, they had her back, they were the wind beneath her wings.

The last bell rang and the Group picked itself off the shady bit of grass they had settled down on for their meeting. Noor lingered. She didn't want to go home. She hated the sound of that last bell—the you-can-go-home-now dong of it—the joyous cries of the younger students spilling out, the happy faces of the seniors making their dignified way to the buses with a less dignified skip in their step. Everyone had a refuge, a place to be—even Sanvi, as much as she grumbled, was probably looking forward to her mother's cooking, sitting at her desk to do her homework, the teasing of her twin cousins when they got back from their schools . . . at least Sanvi knew what to *expect*.

2

The worst thing about this whole horrible thing was not knowing what to anticipate. Ammi had gone, Dad was silent as a tomb and then, last weekend, her father's mother—Daadima to her face, Hateful Old Crone (HOC) behind her back—had moved in to 'help out'.

'I don't need any help,' Noor had informed her father on Friday night. He was going to go to the station the next morning to pick up the HOC.

'Some people like their grandmothers,' said Mr Rai, absently pulling at his beard.

'Some people have *nice* grandmothers.'

'She's old, Noorie, she's set in her ways. But she wants very much to help. I think that's a good sign, don't you?'

Dad had not spoken properly to his mother since he had decided to run off with *Noor's* mother. He had tried, over the years, to keep in touch—sending messages through his younger brother and sister, between whose houses the HOC oscillated—and he had gone to cremate his father when Noor was only two, but whatever had happened at that meeting was never mentioned in their house.

Still, despite the years of not talking, despite the years the HOC had made her father feel horrible and less-than and how-dare-he, the prospect of her arrival made him look happier than he had seemed since Noor's Ammi had left.

Which struck Noor as singularly unfair—why did he get to live with his mother when *her* mother had left?

The list of the things the HOC had already done to prove herself worthy of the title of HOC was long but, in Noor's mind, as she walked up to her front door, it could be classified into two major faults.

Number one: Since the arrival of the HOC—actually, since a little before the arrival of the HOC—Noor had had to give up her bedroom on the lower level of their duplex flat. It was a great bedroom. Noor loved it. It was far away enough from her parents' bedroom that she could play loud music into the night and have her friends over to stay and its proximity to the kitchen meant that she could get a middle-of-the-night snack without waking anyone up and so there was no one to ask, 'Didn't you have enough dinner?' or 'Why are you still awake?'. She had had the room painted her favourite colours at thirteen—lavender walls and a yellow ceiling—and thankfully, she hadn't yet acquired *new* favourite colours to take their place. Her room was marked up with photos of both One Direction (that Zayn, though) and old-school bands like No Doubt (Gwen Stefani had the look Noor always aspired to have) and a poster of the Beatles she just really liked because of the way it looked.

Her bed was angled perfectly after years of research—no light hitting her face in the mornings and in direct contact with the blast of the AC.

Now, Noor and her things had been shunted into the upstairs guest bedroom, right next to the master bedroom, which was not only *smaller* than her old space, it also had boring white walls. 'We'll paint it again,' said Mr Rai, but that wasn't the *point*, Dad. The point was to have everything the same as before. New lavender and yellow paint would not turn this new, imposter room into her old one, which had felt like a friend each time she went in and closed the door. More and more, in the months her mother had been shouting at her father, and voices were raised till they cracked, Noor had retreated, turned up the music as high as it would go and gazed at the bottom of Zayn Malik's chin—the perfect amount of stubble—and imagined pushing that one stubborn lock of hair out of his eyes. For a joke present, Armana had printed out a bunch of Zayn's Instagram photos and put them in a collage to give to Noor, but Noor had hung it up right next to her pillow, without any irony at all, where she could gaze at him every night. Of course, Armana was a Harry Styles girl—'So much more manly than that *chikna* Zayn, plus he, like, *left* them, which is totally not cool, Noor. You've got to give up on him.' But Noor had read about Yoko Ono and John Lennon and that's how she felt about herself and Zayn. Meant to be. She had some Pakistani in her own blood, so his dad would be okay with it.

Those were the things she thought about, while upstairs, the ceiling shook with the force of a slammed door.

Number two on the list of the heinous deeds of the HOC: The moment she came in on Saturday morning, she looked at Noor and her expression wasn't that of someone greeting their long-lost granddaughter whom they had never met.

'This is Noor, Mummyji,' said Dad, pushing Noor forward. Noor had, without being asked, put on a pair of tights and a loose T-shirt, not her usual Saturday morning slob outfit of shorts and a tank top. 'Say Namaste, Noor,' he said, glancing at her.

Noor let the corners of her mouth rise up. 'Namaste,' she said.

'You called her Noor?' said the HOC in Hindi to Mr Rai. 'Outlandish name. As if the child won't have enough problems.'

'Now, Mummyji,' said Dad, laughing nervously, 'We've spoken about this.'

'Chosen by the girl's mother, no doubt, that bloodsucking demon.' The HOC examined Noor closely. 'She's taken after her mother also. But she has our colouring, for that you should be relieved.'

Noor glanced at her father for a cue. Was she just supposed to stand here and be analyzed? Obviously, because he was shaking his head at her to be quiet. And she hadn't even *said* anything yet.

'I wrote to you when she was born,' said the HOC. 'You should have named her Divya.'

Divya? VOM.

'Let us show you your room, Mummyji,' said Dad rapidly, before Noor could make her outrage known. 'We moved Noor's things out of her bedroom on this floor so it would be easier for you.'

'As long as it has a place for me to say my prayers in, beta, I'm okay,' said the HOC, sighing deeply. 'I am an old woman. I do not have any needs, but I'm here to make sure you live a pious life.'

It had only been three days, but the HOC had adhered to this mission statement. Around Noor's home, things were popping up that she had never seen before. The room with the washing machine got a shelf with a silver idol of Krishna playing the flute. Pictures of Ganesha and Rama and Lakshmi came out of fragrant old newspapers from the HOC's battered suitcase and lined the kitchen shelves—the spice jars pushed into one corner to make space for them. Every morning when Noor plodded downstairs for some milk coffee, she smelled the incense before she saw her grandmother and heard the chiming of her small prayer bell.

She had poked her head into her old bedroom to see what changes the HOC had made, when she was spotted and made to sit down in front of a giant idol of Vishnu. How many gods did the HOC have in her bag anyway? She was like some crazy, super-religious Mary Poppins.

The HOC made her cover her head and sit down while she waved incense around and muttered her prayers. 'Say it after me or you'll never learn,' she said, reciting the Gayatri Mantra like it was a holy sacrament she could pour over Noor's head and rid her of every part of her past. 'I blame your father. He should have taught you these things. But he's a man . . . they don't think it's so important.'

'Da-haaa-d,' Noor faced her father later, nostrils flaring, eyes wide.

'She's just trying to settle in, Noorie,' Mr Rai had said, studiously avoiding eye contact. 'She means well. Just ignore the things you don't agree with. I do.'

Having his mother there had changed her father already, though. He spoke less—he hadn't ever been much of a talker, but Noor remembered when it was the three of them, her and her mother and her father, how her mother could tease an opinion out of her father and how he used to laugh. Dad didn't laugh anymore but at least he had stopped retiring to his room and coming out with a red nose and swollen eyes. He was less caustic with his opinions and his voice turned gentle when he spoke to his mother. She'd say something awful, something truly *regressive*, like how all Muslims should convert to Hinduism or leave the country or something, and he'd say, 'Achcha, Mummyji?' and his eyebrows would quirk at Noor like they were sharing a joke—look at this one with her opinions, *so cute*—and Noor wanted to throw her scrambled eggs at him. It wasn't *cute*. It was *awful*. And why was the HOC *here* in her *home* with her dreadful thoughts and her almost constant sniffles and her habit of watching Hindi soaps with the volume turned up because she was going deaf—and cutting vegetables at the same time! Like this was one of *those* households instead of the lovely cosmopolitan home they used to have?

Her life was turning into Sanvi's, and she knew the way the rest of the Group spoke about Sanvi's life when she wasn't there because Noor had once been a participant in such a discussion. 'Poor Sanvi,' one of them would say, and this would be a cue for the rest of them to say, 'Yeah, and did you hear about what her awful sister-in-law did *now*?' or 'Yeah, and she almost got *caught* the last time she went out with Aryan,' and it would all end with one of them saying, 'God, I would *die* if I had the same kind of family.' Then they'd turn silent and inward-thinking and shake their heads. Poor Sanvi. Poor, poor Sanvi.

Now it would turn into poor Noor.

Noor was used to letting herself into her own house—at fourteen, her mother had given her a sterling silver keychain with her very own key on it. 'Now, remember, Noor,' Ammi had said, 'no one comes in before Radha Didi returns at four. After Radha Didi is back, you send her to open the door. You don't open the door. Not even if it's a courier person and you've been waiting for a package delivery for a *week*. You say, 'No one is at home'—*through* the door, not opening it and standing there in your shorts—and you send them next door. They'll collect your parcel for you and give it to Radha Didi when she rings.' These rules were normal. All her friends had some variant of them ever since that poor girl had died in the news, when a man, supposedly there to service her Aquaguard, had raped her and killed her in her very own bedroom.

But Noor loved being in the house by herself. The first thing she would do was run to her room, like a guided missile through the flat, and then close the door firmly behind her. Then she'd turn on the AC (or the heater in winter) and dump her schoolbag on the ground. She would strip off her sweaty uniform and get into something cool—a tank top and a pair of pyjamas or denim shorts and a T-shirt—and make her way to the kitchen, where there'd be a note in her mother's handwriting—she usually wrote it before she left for work at the publishing house she was an editor at. Generally, it was stuck to the microwave and it said something like, 'Noorie, there's a plate for you in the fridge, stick it in the microwave when you get in. MANGOES. Have a great day! Love you.' The choice of fruit in capital letters would change depending on what month it was. Noor normally wouldn't bother with the dining table, even though it was set with a placemat and a fork and spoon for her. Instead, she'd zap her plate and carry it to her room, already blissfully cool (or warm, depending on the time of year), and turn on her laptop, where she would have downloaded the latest TV show she was watching. With the show on and her feet up and her plate of food in front of her, Noor was the happiest she ever was. Later, sometimes, she'd take a nap, and by the time she emerged again, Radha Didi, their housekeeper and her nanny since she was a little girl, would already be there and her milk coffee would be ready and she would carry that to her room and do her homework, before she settled down to the serious business of Group co-ordination for whatever plans they had that week. The Group took academics lightly but they had a no-phone-calls-before-six policy, 'because we want to get into good colleges,' Armana had said when she enforced this. So every evening, all five girls would check their clocks and work hard till 6 p.m. or risk being left out of the evening con-call.

The evening con-call was usually a continuation of what they had talked about in school, and sometimes it could be hard to get a word in edgeways with everyone giggling and chattering at once. It had begun a year ago, when they all got their own cell phones, and they would take turns making calls so that no one person had to pay all the bills.

Noor liked to think of them all in their rooms as they chatted, arranged just so, one biting her lip, one about to say something, her eyes sparkling, one playing with a bit of her hair . . .

Armana would be in her very cool, adult room painted in shades of pale pink and beige. Armana's mother was a famous interior designer and she changed up all the rooms in her house every year and then had a 'New Design Party!' which was one of the funnest events at Armana's house.

Armana's own personal taste had taken a cue from her mum, so everything was muted and girly—a vase of pale silk roses on her white distressed desk, a bulletin board by the door with her 'dream desires', which featured mainly pictures of beautiful women from fashion magazines wearing structured gowns, or cradling expensive bags. In one corner was a leaf-green cabinet where Armana's books lived. Mostly textbooks—she wasn't much of a reader. And under her bed, in big wicker boxes, were the *Vogue* magazines she had been subscribing to since she was twelve. At thirteen, Armana had decided she was too old for dolls and stuffed animals and all those things had gone into storage somewhere in their large house. The only thing left was a pink bear with a heart-shaped nose, a present from her current boyfriend Reansh. She called the bear Monsieur Bear and pretended a French accent for it sometimes when she was feeling goofy. Armana goofy was a lovely sight, almost like something made for television, with her very long hair piled up on top of her head and her very short shorts tight across her pert bottom. Armana could be in one of her magazine ads any time she liked. Hers was a kind of effortless beauty, Noor thought—something the rest of them tried to emulate but could never get close to.

Now, Natasha's room, in contrast, was large and bare, with a double bed she had inherited from her grandfather, and posters of bands all over the chipped walls. Natasha's biggest decoration was the special chest of drawers she'd had made to store CDs—'I know it's old school but sometimes CDs work better than mp3s'—painted black and covered in neon spray paint, spelling out the names of her favourite DJs and song lyrics. Natasha would be lying across her bed as she spoke, kicking at the wall with one bare foot, while the other kept time across her knee to whatever music she had on. While Noor's home ritual was AC, schoolbag, change, fridge, Natasha's was music, AC, schoolbag. She knew what she wanted to listen to all the time and when she wasn't listening to her friends talk, she had noise-cancelling headphones on and was twiddling through her playlist with an expression of concentration on her face. Whenever Noor thought of Natasha, she conjured up that exact face—a thin line appearing between her eyebrows, her mouth a bit pursed in concentration, her eyes darting around as she waited for the first beats of the song to release into her ears and then her expression of relaxation when it was the right song. 'You pick a song like you have to poop,' Noor had once teased her, and Natasha had laughed right back, 'It's the same feeling of relief, yeah!'

Natasha was not as beautiful as Armana—none of them were—but love made Noor think she was gorgeous in her own right. She had a round face, long, shaggy hair streaked pink at the tips and a smile that wrapped right round her head. Her eyes were perhaps her best feature, a throwback from some marauding ancestor, all grey and hazel. 'God, I'd *kill* for your eyes,' Armana would say to Natasha in moments where they pretended they were all the same level of pretty.

Sonum's room was almost exactly the same aesthetic as Armana's, except for one wallpapered wall with bunches of flowers repeating, which she thought was so 'chick', until, giggling, the girls corrected her pronunciation. Sonum wasn't People Like Us in the same way Sanvi wasn't, but Sanvi was friends with them because she lived on Armana's street. Sonum lived all the way in West Delhi in a massive house that looked like a cake, with her own 'sweet' of rooms and the fanciest bathroom Noor had ever seen. Sonum also had a walk-in closet and a dressing table surrounded by bright lights and her name spelt out in glitter on one of the walls. But mostly, what you noticed about Sonum's room was the wall filled with photographs and mementos of the five of them. Sonum was like the group historian, and sometimes, the only one who cared enough about their mall outing or a movie they watched or a sleepover to document it.

Whenever Noor thought of Sonum, she'd feel first an involuntary stab of irritation, which she quickly tried to push away—it's just that she *tried* so hard, and yet, Sonum herself was so lovely. She'd be talking to them while painting her nails or eating something her cook would bring in, and her lips would be very highly glossed—they always were—and her hair would fall stick straight and shiny across her shoulders and she'd look smooth and buttery and rich and yet, not sexy or luxe or desirable. Her father was in 'bizness', her mother was a homemaker who was very involved in the West Delhi socialite scene and they also had a farmhouse on the outskirts of Delhi, with a pool where the girls spent most of their summers.

And finally Sanvi, who probably wasn't in her room at all, unless she had it to herself, because she had to share it with a younger cousin. Sanvi took herself and her cell phone for her evening walk, with the claim that she needed to 'reduce', bought herself two cigarettes from the local shop and spent her evenings in a park two blocks down, smoking them and then rubbing a small blue packet of supari called *Chutki* all over her fingers to get rid of the smell. *Chutki* had a miraculous ability to hide the smell of smoke, apparently. Sanvi's nails were bitten to the quick but painted black, her thick, straight hair, cut in a bob, fell across her face—'How did you get away with it?' the girls had asked, clamouring, when she first went to school like that. 'Oh, I just went and had it cut and went home and then they couldn't say anything,' Sanvi had said coolly. Sanvi was easily the coolest person Noor could think of, family background or not, and the few times she had been over there for lunch, she had been almost disoriented to hear Sanvi's smoky, gravelly voice become demure, saying, 'Yes, Ma' and 'No, Ma' and on and on, till Noor had lifted her head and gazed right at Sanvi and Sanvi had winked, like, *don't pay attention, I'm only acting* and Noor had felt reassured that her world was secure.

No matter whose house was the fanciest (Sonum's) or the coolest (Armana's) or where there were the fewest rules (Natasha's) or where the food was excellent (Sanvi's), the Group liked to gather at Noor's at least once a month. 'When are you having us over, Noor?' Armana would ask and the others would say, 'Yes, Noor, it's been *ages*', and Noor would go home and ask her mother and the two of them would plan for a Sunday brunch or a Friday dinner, always around when Ammi was free because that's who the girls really came to see.

Noor's mum was the *best* mum. She didn't judge them for any of their rebellions, though she did tell Sanvi gently that smoking would give her early wrinkles and Sanvi hadn't snuck off at all after that for a cigarette. She listened to boy trouble and teacher trouble and advised them very maturely on what to do, just as if they were adults themselves. They called her 'Khala' to her face, because that's what she preferred to 'Aunty', but they called her Roxy behind her back because that's what Noor's dad and everyone else called her. Roxy was short for Ruxana. Roxy Khala, Rox, Roxette. 'I miss Rox, Noor!' Sanvi would poke her with the tip of her ballet flat. 'I need some safe-sex advice!'

*

'Gudiya, is that you?'

Noor's usual homecoming routine? Yup, that had all vanished since the HOC rode into town on that Shatabdi and ruined her life.

'Gudiya'? The HOC disliked the name 'Noor' so much, she chose to call her 'doll'. Small, plastic and passive—the HOC's ideal granddaughter.

Noor sighed, left her bag on the floor and went into her old room / the HOC's current Home of Hindu Piousness. Her grandmother was sitting on the bed, shelling peas, with a large book Noor recognized as the battered old Bhagavadgita that she always seemed to be reading in her downtime.

'I need someone to turn the pages,' the HOC said. 'Go wash your hands and come and help me. That maid of yours—I don't know what your mother was thinking, letting her run free like that—but she never comes before five. It's ridiculous. Now, in your Chacha's home . . .'

Noor tuned out at this point. In her father's younger brother's home, which was where the HOC had come from, everything was perfect and nothing sucked. In her Chacha's home, the maids kowtowed to the HOC every morning and never needed to be told what to do. In her Chacha's home, his wife listened to the HOC and took her decisions to be next only to God's. In her Chacha's home, his two young children finished their homework and then spent their time listening to stories their grandmother told them and never even thought of locking themselves up inside their rooms to do God-knows-what.

Noor suspected the HOC thought she was doing far

worse than actually talking on the phone. Smoking, maybe. That would be bad. Or the thing where she ran her hand over her stomach and then put it into her underpants. That was something she didn't tell anyone about but the HOC could see it all in her face. 'This city is full of sin,' the HOC would say meaningfully, and Noor's father would nod absently, but Noor would catch her gimlet eye. 'Full. Of. Ssssin.' The HOC would repeat sibilantly, just so Noor got whose sin they were talking about.

'I can't turn the pages for you, Daadi,' said Noor, in her Reasonable Voice, 'I'm going to go eat lunch.'

'Of course,' said the HOC. 'But food for the soul is also food for the stomach. Never mind, child, it's not your fault. Your mother's people put pleasure over duty.'

Noor gritted her teeth and smiled again, 'I'm going to go to my room now, Daadi,' she said. If she lost her temper, she would be no less than the people her grandmother thought she was one of. Besides, it gave her a certain sense of satisfaction to see her grandmother's face look expectant of a temper tantrum and then be disappointed. The wrinkles sort of started up and then sagged. Noor liked when the HOC's wrinkles sagged. It meant things hadn't gone the way she had wanted them to.

The whole problem the HOC had with Ammi was that Ammi was Muslim. Now, the Khans, Ammi's family, were a fairly liberal lot. They were from Bombay. They let Ammi and her two sisters do what they liked and didn't insist on prayers or anything. Noor's father had migrated to Bombay from Jaipur with his first job and had met Ammi, a young intern ('the only time I tried banking to please my father, and I hated it!'), and had fallen madly in love. The Khans had sort of adopted Mr Rai once they figured their Roxy wasn't going to give him up and he began to already be a son-in-law before he actually became one.

'Then what, Ammi?' Noor used to ask, when she was a little girl.

'Then he said, "Oh, I have to go back to Jaipur, my mother isn't well," and I said, "Are you going to tell her about us?" and he looked shifty and I knew he wasn't going to.' Ammi didn't mince her words even then. She thought Noor should know the true and honest answer to every question she asked.

'And then you said . . . ?'

'And then I said, "Listen, you." Here, Noor would burst into giggles at the thought of her father being 'you' and Ammi would grin. 'I said, "Listen, you, if you don't tell her and you come back here like a *dog*—"'

'With his tail between his legs!' Noor would finish for her, crowing.

Her father, if he was listening, would harrumph and shake his newspaper and say, 'Are you sure you should be telling her these stories, Roxy?'

And her mother would say, 'Why not? It's true, isn't it?'

And her father would be defeated by True Isn't It and would retreat again and her mother would go on. 'And you come back like a dog with his tail between his legs, I will never, ever, *ever* talk to you again. We are finished, Vivek Rai! Finished *forever!*'

Noor would hold her breath. So close she had come to not being born.

'And then he said, "Well, I was going to wait till I saw my mother, Rox, but since you insist."'

'And then he got down on one knee!'

'Not quite. His knees were already giving him trouble.' This, with an arch glance at Noor's dad.

'But he whipped out a ring,' Noor prompted.

'He *whipped* out a ring from his shirt pocket and he said, "Ruxana, will you marry me?"'

'And you said yes!' This was the point Noor would glance down at her mother's hands, usually doing something while she was telling the story—holding a book, or folding some clothes or knitting (she loved to knit)—and see the thin gold band with a tiny diamond that her lovesick father had given her mother all those years ago. Sometimes, her mother would take it off and let Noor wear it and Noor would pretend to be a big lady with an engagement ring or a millionaire dripping with diamonds, and her mother would put down her work and walk across the room and kiss her father on the head so softly but with so much love that Noor longed to be a grown up right then so she could have that too.

Only much later had Noor thought to ask what happened after. This time, her mother had put aside the crossword she was doing and folded her hands in her lap. 'His mother wasn't pleased, Noorie,' she said, looking at Noor with great love and kindness.

'But why not?' Noor asked. 'Your family was rich.' A classmate of hers had just announced that her brother was marrying a woman with a much lower income than his and how his family was very upset, and now Noor associated a bad marriage with someone having lesser money than the other.

'It wasn't the money,' Noor's mother looked at her very hard, like she was trying to explain something difficult. 'It was because we are Muslim.'

Noor puzzled it over for a bit. She knew the word and she knew it somehow meant something bad because that was what some people had said at school, but it had never been brought up before, not in her home, not in her grandparents' sunny Bombay flat where they went some summers.

'What *exactly* is a Muslim, Ammi?'

At this, Ammi laughed and Noor was insulted, but her mother was quick to add, 'I'm just laughing out of relief, Noorie! A Muslim is someone who worships Allah, just as Hindus have all their gods. You know them—Ganesha and Lakshmi and all that lot?' Noor nodded. 'And a Christian worships Jesus and Buddhists don't actually believe in a God at all . . . but what makes me laugh now is that your father's mother was so scared that her grandchildren would grow up Muslim that she never spoke to your father again, and here you are, asking me what a Muslim is.'

'I think I'd like to be a Buddhist,' Noor said, after some thought.

'Do it,' said her mother, picking up the crossword again. 'You can be whatever you want to be, Noor, and no one can ever bully you out of that.'

'So,' Noor said, just to be clear, 'everyone's always fighting because they think their gods are better? That's kinda stupid.'

'You said it, *meri jaan*.'

3

'I think I've decided on Prateek for my boyfriend,' Natasha said, tugging on a piece of her hair, the way she did when she wanted to sound super casual but was actually nervous.

The Group was sitting around by the ice-cream cart in the school cafeteria and watching a gang of boys roughhouse amongst themselves. Probably for their benefit. Boys tended to get louder around the Group, jumping to show how athletic they were, pitching their voices lower so they'd sound deep, splashing themselves with cologne till the halls were a fugue of Issey Miyake or whatever they were using.

'Prateek, huh?' Armana looked hard at the boys. 'He's a football player, right? Not bad.'

'Yeah, he's not bad,' said Sonum, tugging on her skirt so it covered her thighs, which she was very self-conscious about. She glanced at Armana, 'Quite cute, too.'

Natasha and Noor exchanged glances and Noor rolled her eyes comically. They mocked Sonum's habit of always copying Armana. 'If Armana said VIP chaddis were cool,

Sonum would run right out and buy ten *thousand*,' Natasha would giggle.

Noor glanced towards where the boys had now scattered, and Prateek, unaware of the great honour that had just been granted to him, was drinking water from a bottle, his throat moving, his head tilted back, the water pouring into his mouth. She decided she liked the curve of his jaw and his very curly hair. Having a boyfriend was a recent social necessity of belonging. One day they were all fourteen, and everyone was disgusted with the opposite sex—the way they *smelled*, the way they *talked*—and almost the next minute, everyone was batting their eyelashes and brushing their hair around them with the low, long strokes you would associate with grooming a horse, and school parties, boisterous affairs with pizza and games, turned into music-dance parties. Someone played a slow song and you detached yourself from your friends and, stammering and shy, a boy approached you and you twined your arms around his neck and swayed in time to the music. If he liked you a lot, you'd start 'going around', and then you'd spend half your time discussing him and the other half actually spending time with him.

Armana, the first to do everything, had been the first to have a boyfriend, the gentle Anirudh, who was three years their senior and who insisted on keeping her bracelet in his shirt pocket during his board exams for good luck. Almost as soon as his exams were over, Armana had dropped him speedily for the new boy in school, Reansh, whose spiky hair and crooked smile were so much cooler than poor Anirudh. Anirudh had moped for a while, calling the whole group to talk about her, much to their delight, and to Armana's, because she loved drama. Reansh was more than a match for her, though. It was widely agreed that he was the best-looking boy in school, and Armana took a certain pleasure from walking him through corridors to show him off. Now he was coming towards them, and Noor—always curious about how a girlfriend should behave—glanced at Armana. As always, her friend was the master of her emotions and she pretended like she didn't even see Reansh, but her laugh got louder and she did the thing where she bit her bottom lip, as if overcome by emotion, and let her eyes dance and flipped her hair, and then, when Reansh said, 'Boo!' into her ear, she squealed and slapped him on the shoulder.

'What are you guys talking about?' asked Reansh, nodding at them. Sometimes, Noor felt that Reansh was actually a forty-year-old pretending to be a teenager. He was so cool, so suave, so unnerved by it all, like some teen from a TV show. She had tried once to imagine him farting or picking his nose, but the images refused to form. Reansh was above it all, and so he always reduced her to giggles.

Natasha, nostrils flared, tried to shake her head at Armana, but Armana went on blithely, 'Oh, we were talking about Natasha's new *crush.*' Natasha looked like she wanted to be dead and buried. She was a very private person and seldom said much about her own emotions. Noor realized with a shock that if Natasha cared so much about what Armana said, then she probably really liked this Prateek guy. She felt a bit hurt that Natasha hadn't said anything to her privately. The two of them were closer to each other than anyone else in the Group, so they normally shared information like this before they told the others.

'Who's the lucky guy, music genius?' asked Reansh, lazily, glancing up at where Natasha was sitting on the stair above him.

'No one,' muttered Natasha, but Armana laughed and said, 'Don't *lie*, Nuts! It's that guy Prateek. Rey-rey, you know him?'

'Prateek? Yeah, I know him. We play basketball together at the court near my house. He's cool. Good taste, Natasha.'

'See, I told you,' said Armana smugly, like she had invented Prateek. 'Now, Rey-rey, since you know him, you've gotta call him for the party we're having this weekend. It'll be so awesome if you start dating, Nuts, we can like double-date.' She tossed a glance at Sanvi. 'No offense, Sanster, but your boyfriend doesn't really have much in common with the rest of us.' She muffled a snort of laughter, making it sound like she wanted all of them to hear it.

Sanvi just shrugged and said, 'None taken,' but Noor knew she must be really hurt.

The bell rang and Natasha got up like she had been waiting for it to ring for a really long time. Which she probably had. 'I've got to get to class,' she said. 'Coming, Noor?' Noor rose obediently and scurried off behind Natasha, leaving the rest laughing and calling, 'OOOOOOOOH.'

'Ugh, I shouldn't have said anything,' said Natasha as soon as they were out of earshot.

'You really shouldn't have,' said Noor. 'And um, hello, how long has this been going on?'

'There's no *this*. I've just been . . . noticing him.'

'You know how those sports types are, they have no brain. He'll probably call you "bebe" or something.'

Noor thought Natasha would laugh along with her. How often had the two of them mocked all the sports players in their school. 'Troglodytes,' Natasha would say, and Noor would add, 'Braaaaainsssss. I want braaaaains.'

But instead, Natasha paused by the girl's loo and said, her eyes brimming with angry tears, 'Thanks for being on *my* side.' And then she went in, closing the door firmly behind her, leaving Noor even more confused than before.

An email from Noor's mother that morning:

My very dearest little Noorie,

I tried to call you a few days ago, but then I heard an unfamiliar voice say 'hello'. I asked to speak to you and the voice said you weren't there, you were in school or not yet home or something. 'Ask her to call me back,' I said, but since I haven't heard from you, I'm assuming you either haven't received the message—and we know the voice (if it is who I'm thinking) is capable of that—or that you are still angry with me.

I'm not sure which option is worse: on the one hand, I don't want you to think that in all this, my thoughts have left you. Actually, I have thought of nothing BUT you. I was saying to Sunny Uncle the other day at breakfast (We are in a lovely hotel in Paris, you would love this city. I'm saving up all the nice things for us to do together.) that it didn't feel like a proper breakfast without you here to admire the croissants, or steal away little pots of jam to eat later. He said we should bring you here SOON and I agree with him and I'm working on it, my Noorie.

On the other hand, if you are still angry with me, then I don't blame you. It's hardest on you, all this change, I know. And it had NOTHING to do with you. I know I've said that before, but I want to keep saying it till you understand: events happened in a strange way, and my life changed, and as a result, all of our lives changed. None of this was planned, but what has not changed is my love for you. I miss you every day. When you forgive me—and I won't say 'if' but 'when', and hope—then I want to tell you all about my new life—and yours! It will all be yours.

Hold on hard and be strong, my love. It will all be better soon.

With all the love in the world,

Ammi

As they were leaving their last class of the day, (Natasha had gone in by herself and sat down at a desk with Joy Mukherjee, who wore his pants around his waist and blinked owlishly whenever you asked him a question. Noor, entering later, having counselled Sonum through a hair crisis, had no one to sit with. So she sat by herself at the back, Natasha immune to her pleading looks.) Saras Ma'am, their school counsellor and an all-round cool person, caught Noor before she reached the gate. 'Noor Khan Rai!' she said, grinning from her office door. 'Just the person I wanted to see. Would you pop in here for a second, dear?' Noor had been despondently walking alone—Natasha's embargo on all things Noor seemed to extend to waiting for her as they both left their last class together and, as soon as the bell rang, she had zoomed out of the door. The other three were in Humanities and didn't have a last period, so they had probably left ages ago, to stop at the nearby market for coffee or go home.

She was actually glad for a distraction, so she entered Saras Ma'am's cosy little office, the walls painted a deep mustard yellow—which was prettier than it sounded—lots of carpets and floor cushions, and only one desk in the corner, 'to dump my things, not because I'm a teacher,' Saras Ma'am always said.

Truth be told, Noor had always been a little jealous of the others because in Humanities you could do Psychology, which Saras Ma'am taught. She also led workshops for the younger classes, which is where Noor and the others had met her for the first time and had all turned completely devoted to her cause. Saras Ma'am was cool—she wore interesting, edgy clothes, which still somehow conformed to the 'teacher dress code'. Saras Ma'am was young—she couldn't have been more than twenty-seven or twenty-eight. Saras Ma'am had a boyfriend who picked her up some days on his Enfield. Saras Ma'am got down on the floor with you and encouraged you to talk about your feelings. She said things like, 'I've always got your back' and 'Make good choices, guys!'

'Noor.' Saras Ma'am stood smiling at her for a second, and Noor smiled back. You couldn't help it. She had this big, beautiful grin that stretched from ear to ear and you sort of wanted to make her happy and see her use it. 'Sit, sit,' said her teacher. 'You won't miss the bus yet, you have about fifteen minutes.'

Noor remained standing, though, and shifted her backpack from one shoulder to the other.

'I spoke to your mother, Noor,' said Saras Ma'am, tilting her head and looking at her.

Noor felt her face freeze. She kept her shoulders very level and moved her feet so they were parallel to each other.

'She told me to check in on you, see if you were okay.' Saras Ma'am looked very intently at Noor's face. 'Are you okay? These things are hard.'

Noor managed a shrug.

'I want you to join this after-school club I'm starting.' Saras Ma'am rifled through some papers on her desk and pulled out a violet flyer, handing it to Noor.

Divorced parents getting you down?
Do you feel all alone?
Do you feel like no one understands the situation you're in?
Join the Teens of Divorce (TOD) club and meet other people in the same situation as you!
Totally anonymous!
Extra-credit assignments!
Stop by the school counsellor's office for more information and a parent permission slip!
Open to all, and no judgement!

Noor looked at it and tried to hand it back. 'Thanks,' she said. There was a frog in her throat, so she had to clear it a few times. She tried again, 'Thanks, but I don't need it.'

'Maybe *you* don't but perhaps you can help other people?' Saras Ma'am suggested. 'Not everyone is as fortunate to have such a lovely group of friends as you do.'

'I don't think so,' said Noor, edging towards the door.

'Noor.'

Noor looked up.

'Come for the first one. It's tomorrow,' Saras Ma'am touched her lightly on the shoulder. 'It's not optional. I'd really like for you to attend, and your mother has already okay-ed it.'

And then the final bell to signal the buses leaving rang, and Noor got out of the office in a sprint, still clutching the flyer in her hand.

The HOC was in full form by the time Noor got home. She had noticed her father's car in his parking space, which was a surprise, because he normally got in only by about eight. Radha Didi opened the door for Noor—another surprise—but she didn't even smile in response to Noor's namaste. Instead, she took Noor's schoolbag with a face like Droopy Dog and shuffled away, looking more and more hard done by. Noor could hear her mutter, as she walked off, 'All the thanks I get' and 'For twelve years I worked with this family' and 'Just walks right in here and thinks she's the queen of the world'.

'Do I even want to know?' Noor asked herself, but she knew she didn't have much of a choice.

'Is that Gudiya?' called the HOC's even HOC-er voice.

'Gudiyaaaaaa, come here!'

Noor presented herself at the doorway of her old room, where her father was tapping away on his phone and the HOC turned beady eyes on her.

'My name. Is. Noor.'

The HOC waved her sentence away. 'Gudiya, go have a bath really quickly. Your father has something to say to you.' She poked at Noor's dad, 'Tell her, beta.'

'Beta' looked up from his phone, looking harried. 'Ah. Noor. Did you have lunch?'

Noor rolled her eyes. Her father trying to be father-like and enquiring after her well-being was hypocritical since obviously, no one cared about what she thought about things.

'I just got home, Dad,' she said.

'Oh yes, of course.' Long pause. Her father pulled on his beard.

'Listen, I've got homework,' Noor said. 'You guys just *call* me in here and you don't say anything.'

This whole conversation was going on in English and the HOC was popping candied supari into her mouth and watching them like a jungle babbler looking at a worm.

'I don't know what you two are saying,' she said, 'but Gudiya, today is your grandfather's death anniversary.'

'Oh,' said Noor. Then, seeing there was a greater response expected from her, she said, 'I'm sorry?'

The HOC looked impatient. 'Obviously, she does not know what that means,' she said to her son. 'Why am I even surprised? That woman ran your house like some kind of . . . I-don't-know-what! Thank *God* I looked at my almanac. Thank *God*. Or else your poor father. Restless and wondering why his son has forsaken him.'

Her rheumy eyes filled with tears. Noor was not alarmed. The HOC periodically let her eyes fill with tears. It seemed like something she had on tap. She hoped her father wouldn't rise to the bait.

Too late. He had taken her hand and was patting her on the back. 'There, there, Mummyji,' he said. 'Of course no one is forsaken.'

Noor remembered very vividly how, at eight, she had been very alarmed that they wouldn't go to heaven because none of them prayed. She had been practically hysterical about it. A Catholic friend had told her the only way to go to heaven was by accepting Jesus Christ and did she want to wander *alone* for the rest of her *life* without her mummy and daddy because they didn't take the appropriate precautions?

'Now, when I'm dead,' Mary Ann had said smugly, 'I'll be with my mummy–daddy, my grandparents, my sister and my brother and we'll have a happy family in heaven. *Forever.*'

Noor had been so upset by this that she had cried the rest of the evening, with her mother stroking her hair and saying, 'There, there, of course we'll go to heaven! We'll just go to a heaven without all those Jesus types! We'll hang out with Marilyn Monroe and Mahatma Gandhi and have them all over to our heaven house.' And she had been just on the brink of accepting this as a greater fate, when her father had heard all this and rumbled, 'Nonsense! Have a scientific mind, Noor! There is no heaven! When we die, we rot and our bodies become food, unless you're cremated, in which case you're burned. Either way, there's no other life. There's only this one.'

Noor's tears had started afresh and her mother had turned on her father like a tigress. 'Must you say such cruel things?' Ammi had demanded.

'I must,' said Dad, unmoved. 'Noor has to learn to make the most of this life, the one she has now, because there is no other life.'

And despite tears, he had not budged from his position. The same man who was now trying to comfort his mother about his dead father's soul. Noor sent him a piercing glance, which he looked down with blank innocence.

'Did you eat meat today, Gudiya?' asked the HOC, sniffing loudly and fumbling for the embroidered handkerchief she kept in her blouse.

Noor was about to nod yes—she'd had a mutton Frankie for lunch—but her father was shaking his head at her so vigorously that she shook hers as well.

'Good, then we can do the puja today. My pandit will come soon. It's so hard finding a good pandit, but Rimi ki Ma recommended her sister's fellow. I hope he's good—he's certainly charging enough.'

Her eyes fell on Noor, who was playing with a button on her shirt.

'Go have a bath, Gudiya! It's already late for the puja. Hurry up. And don't eat anything.'

Noor turned to leave, hoping her eye roll could be felt like an earthquake inside the room.

'Wait, Gudiya,' the HOC said, suddenly.

'Wha-haa-t?' asked Noor, tired and hungry.

The HOC glanced at Noor's dad, back to looking at his phone, and then beckoned Noor closer. Noor leaned forward with her body, tilting her head back so she didn't have to inhale the HOC odour. But her grandmother had grabbed her shoulder and was pulling her in. Her breath smelled cloying, like the candied supari she chowed down.

'Are you on your time?' she shout-whispered into Noor's ear.

'My what?'

'Your *time*.'

'I don't understand, Daadima.'

'Uff, this girl is *too* stupid.' She turned to Noor's father. 'Beta, ask your daughter if she is pure, if she is clean.'

'I'm *just* going to have a shower!' Noor said.

'Um, she means . . .' The tips of Dad's ears went red. For a beardy man, he had unusual places for his blush. 'She means, do you have your period?'

Noor blushed too. It had always been a woman thing that Ammi and she had shared.

When she first started her period, about four years ago, her mother had made her a now-you-are-a-woman dinner and her father had harrumphed and handed her an envelope with a thousand rupees in it. That night, he had drunk three glasses of wine, and looked lovingly at Noor. 'You know, it's a big responsibility to become a woman, Noorie. You have to be the guardian of your body now.'

'Dad!' Noor had exclaimed, looking at the floor, willing it to open up and swallow her whole, like Sita. Except, Sita probably never had to have this conversation with *her* father. (How did Sita have her period in the forest anyway?)

Since then, her father had never once brought it up, not even when he bought sanitary pads. He just left them on the table for Ammi and Noor to collect. Quietly. As he put away the rest of the groceries. She had always liked that image of her father, going into a store and putting sanitary towels into his shopping basket, perhaps peering at the label over the top of his reading glasses. Coming home and placing the packets on the dining table, probably unwrapped from their newspaper covering that the shop owner would have slipped them in to make them more discreet. They had a blackboard in the kitchen with a running grocery list that either her father or her mother would shop for, and Noor was encouraged to add her own things, 'within reason'.

WHISPER ULTRA THIN WITH WINGS, she'd write, followed by MORE NUTELLA PLEASE? And a smiley face.

Her period had been a woman thing to be shared with her mother, but her father never made her feel awkward or weird about it.

Except for, like, right now.

While sitting in front of a teeny, tiny fire on the balcony, head covered, freshly bathed, denied her cell phone, Noor considered God.

Her grandmother believed in the kind of God who was only happy when appeased. If you believed in the HOC's God, you'd be making sacrifices every month—and not the kind of self-denial sacrifices other religions depended on. The HOC's God needed you to *show* Him how much you loved Him. (Or Her. Or Elephant Boy.) You had to call a special God Spokesperson (in this case, the priest, who was bare-chested and had a rivulet of sweat resting on his rotund belly) and you had to spend money and have just the right kind of things. He was sort of like a holy spirit you invoked through a string of magic words and sweet-smelling smoke. Like magic. If you pleased the HOC's God, He would do things for you, like help your dead grandfather live a good life. If you didn't, then presumably, your dead grandfather would be shunted off to some version of Hindu Hell, forced to suffer because of your callousness.

On the flipside, the God of her other grandparents wasn't much better. You gave up so much, with promises of rewards only in Heaven. No bacon! (Noor had been quite upset when she'd heard that) And the women had to be modest and you had to starve yourself for thirty days or whatever. Although, the plus side to starving yourself was having super-rich breakfasts filled with meat, which the HOC's God would have a fainting spell about.

Then there was her father's God, which was no God at all. If you could see something, it existed, if you didn't, it wasn't there. Unless someone had proven otherwise. Like the Big Bang or the atom or multiple universes, all of which seemed as miraculous and hinging on faith as God did. You could either believe a scientist or you could believe a prophet. At the end of the day, you had to hang your hat on one of those pegs, and while Noor was drawn to her father's theory, it would sometimes be comforting to have a list of rules for life with a promise of a reward if you did things well.

The priest finished his incantations and the fire let out a smoky breath, and Noor glanced at her father to see how he was taking this. To her surprise, he had his head bowed and two tracks of tears made their way down his face. The HOC had noticed too, and she was clutching Dad's hand in hers and looking sorrowful but Noor definitely saw a glimmer of triumph in her eyes. The HOC: 1, Ammi: 0. Actually, Ammi: -25 right now. But Noor didn't allow herself to think about her mother, not when every time she actually thought about her, she felt the sharp prickle of tears up her nose.

She heard the familiar tone of her cell ringing and thought vaguely, 'Oh, it must be six o'clock.' Glancing at her two family members, she decided they wouldn't miss her and darted off inside to her phone and her friends, to her life that was beyond all these adults and the things they made her do and how unhappy they all were.

4

The party was that weekend and that was all the Group had been talking about for the past ten days. Now it was Thursday, and Noor sat in an empty classroom, dangling her legs off a table, while, around her, her friends shouted each other down, accompanied by loud laughter. She allowed herself a moment of joy and anticipation: parties were so, *so* amazing! She would wear a pretty dress—she wasn't sure exactly which yet—and they would all gather at Armana's house early to begin the festivities and the evening would end with them all in Armana's room, the trundle bed pulled out, the fold-out futon made up with floral sheets. That was actually the part of the evening Noor was looking forward to *most*. The end of the evening, with them all wrapping up and winding down, eating the last of the snacks (because the Group didn't eat at parties), doing a debrief of who was there and what was said and what they wore. She hugged herself with joy just as a paper aeroplane flew across the room and hit her on the nose.

'Ow!' she said, more out of surprise than pain.

The others giggled. Sanvi, who had thrown the plane,

said, 'Well, you were off and dreaming, so we just thought we'd bring you back to earth.'

'Seriously, Noor, you've been damn spacey lately,' said Armana.

Noor held her breath, ready to come up with an untrue excuse, but Armana had already moved on, buoyed by the excitement.

'My mother said we can order in. I thought some kebab rolls, some chips.' She checked off the food on her slender fingers, one of which had a ring on it that stopped between her first and second knuckle. 'A midi ring,' she had told Sonum when she admired it. It was shaped like an infinity sign and was small and delicate. All the girls had tried it on but it looked strange and misshapen on their fingers.

'Cupcakes?' asked Armana, and the others nodded, Sonum's tongue swiped her lower lip. 'Okay, okay, Sonum, calm down, girl!' laughed Armana, who missed nothing. 'We'll get you some food, fatty.' The 'fatty' was said low and caressing, with more love than spite, but Noor saw Sonum sit up straighter and suck in her stomach.

'And my guy will make sandwiches.' Armana looked at Sanvi next. 'Your . . . Aryan, will he bring alcohol?' She said 'Aryan' like it hurt her to say it but Sanvi looked back at her placidly. 'Yes,' she said, 'Vodka, beer and some white wine for us. I'll need to give him the money though.'

'Sure. Everyone, give Sanvi some cash. Don't want old Aryan to be broke on account of a bottle of vodka.'

Sometimes, Armana didn't get that people could have less money and still be cool. Actually, that whole concept pretty much flew right over her head. Her world was divided

into People Like Us, who shopped at the right stores and
wore the right labels, and People Like Them, who 'went
dutch' at a coffee shop or said openly that they couldn't
afford something. Especially a boy. If a *boy* said it, he was
out of the dating pool forever.

The funny thing was, Armana rarely paid for things
herself. She had a credit card, which her parents had given
her, with apparently no upper limit, but she didn't use it
very often, unless she was shopping. People were always
buying Armana things or offering to cover her share, as
Sonum did all the time, or just giving her everything she
asked for, like Reansh did. Even now, she sat picking at one
shiny nail as everyone handed over cash to Sanvi, and said,
lazily, 'I think you guys should pay for the booze. I mean,
I'm already providing the place *and* the snacks. If I buy the
booze too, it'll basically be *my* party and we'll have to take
all your names off the host list.'

Noor had not been raised with a heavy allowance but
it was decent, a thousand rupees a week. This she couldn't
exceed, unless it was Special Occasion Shopping, for which
she shortlisted a few clothes, checked out their price tags and
told her parents exactly how much she needed. They also
paid for her phone bill as long as it didn't go over thousand a
month or something. Most stuff she paid for by squirreling
away money. She was a great saver, and the wad of cash
she kept in her secret hiding spot had at least three or four
thousand at any one point for emergencies. It was from
that that she pulled out seven hundred and handed it over
to Sanvi. Sonum and Armana didn't have to account for any
of their money, and Sonum was peeling off two thousand-

rupee notes to give Sanvi, regardless of the fact that that was basically their whole alcohol budget. Sanvi caught Armana's eye and Armana shrugged. More beer, then. Natasha had the same pocket money as Noor but she often didn't save, and so she was placing what looked like only a few hundred, made out of small change, on the table.

'Seriously, Natasha,' protested Sanvi, 'I can't take all those coins!'

'I'm sorry! I only have these. I had to have this new album and my brother would only buy it for me with his card if I promised to pay him back right then.' Natasha was laboriously dividing the coins into piles. 'And . . . two hundred!' She pushed them across the table to Sanvi, who accepted them gingerly.

'And are we done acting like shopkeepers?' asked Armana, who always professed to be hugely bored by cash transactions of any kind. It seemed so cool and above-it-all that Noor had tried to affect the same attitude, transcending it all, on several occasions, but couldn't. You had to be rich to pull it off properly.

'We're done,' said Sanvi, still lightly. Sometimes, Noor wondered about Sanvi. She seemed so cool on the surface, unruffled by all the barbs that Armana handed out, and Noor used to think she was just *like* that, just chill. But since Noor had begun living with the HOC, she practised the same kind of not-engaging warfare and she knew it for what it was—warfare. She knew that the more Sanvi ignored her, the more Armana would pry and poke and try to get a reaction out of her. And she also knew that as long as Sanvi was silent and calm, she was winning.

'Who is coming to the shops then? All of us?' Armana asked, her tone as light and pretty as it always was. If there were cracks, she wasn't showing them.

They all nodded, except Noor. 'I have an after-school thing,' she said, rolling her eyes and trying to look bored. 'Saras Ma'am asked me to come. Some club or the other she's really excited about.'

'Saras is too *cute* with her little passions,' said Armana, 'Okay, go on then, teacher's pet.'

As Noor left the room, she realized that Natasha still hadn't said a word to her. She felt suddenly angry. The rest of the girls had been just as bitchy as she was, if not more. Stupid Natasha. Stupid Saras Ma'am. Everyone was awful and Noor wanted to *die*.

The TOD meeting was held after hours in the music room, a friendly space with a little makeshift stage and lots of nooks and crannies. It was a basement room, and the music teacher Mr Fernandez, had tried to make it a sort of sanctuary. If you were talented, he recruited you and you were his pet, but apart from his special students, the rest of them also did random karaoke afternoons or choir try-outs, where he would patiently play a key over and over again till they got the note right. The music kids held themselves slightly apart—if you could sing or play an instrument, Mr Fernandez would pull you out of class and get you to sit with him almost for the whole day, while he showed other pupils 'how it was done'. Natasha, one of the few aspiring DJs in the school, had, at first, resisted the idea of Mr Fernandez—'He's probably going to be all *traditional* and *boring.*'—but when it was time for her section to have their extra curricular music class, and Mr Fernandez had asked if any of them had an interest in music, she had shot her arm up.

'Play something?' he asked, gesturing towards the guitar and the piano, the sitar and the tabla ready and waiting in case that was her thing. Natasha had shaken her head.

'Sing something, then,' he offered, and she had sighed a deep sigh and said, almost pained, 'I DJ,' waiting for him to dismiss her.

But he hadn't. He had looked thoughtful, and then he'd said, 'I'm assuming you have turntable equipment?' And she had nodded, and he'd said, 'We don't have the budget for that in school but I do have a laptop I'm happy to have you use. Tell me the name of the programme I should get.' And the next time, he offered her the use of his laptop and she did a set, mixing *Wild Thing* with Nusrat Fateh Ali Khan's *Afreen Afreen*, and the class had been unable to sit still, all tapping their feet and moving their bodies, and Mr Fernandez had said, 'Well? Don't just sit there! This is a dance party!'

Noor remembered the expression of pure joy on Natasha's face as she sat on a stool in front of the class, holding the bulky laptop and pulling up songs so that their tempo ran through all the people there, holding up their arms and swinging their hair and acting like they were at a club. Noor had been sort of glad the rest of the Group wasn't in Natasha's and her section; they would undoubtedly think they were too cool to participate in a dorky music-room dance party. But it had made Natasha happy and Mr Fernandez and she were now friends, and often, he took her classes one-on-one, once even asking her if she'd like to conduct a DJ workshop for other kids, which she had joyfully accepted. Sitting in the music room with this new club made her miss Natasha strongly but then she remembered they weren't speaking, so she pushed Natasha firmly out of her mind and walked over to where Saras Ma'am was opening a box of bakery biscuits.

There were two other people there already. A shy looking girl of about twelve, with braids that hung like loops from each side of her head, tied with ribbons that made her look younger than she probably was, and a tall, nondescript boy with glasses, who looked like he was Noor's age. Noor didn't recognize either of them. Their school wasn't a big one, but there were currents in which people moved and you seldom saw people from outside your own particular stream. If you were good at something—sports, perhaps, or acting—then the whole school might know who you were, but most people weren't good at things, so they went along, living parallel lives for the whole of their educational career.

'Noor! Delighted you could join us!' said Saras Ma'am sweetly, as if she hadn't made it mandatory to attend in the first place. Noor gave her a sweet, fake smile back and then hovered by the biscuits.

'Have one! All of you have one. You must be hungry.' The TOD meetings will always have snacks,' said Saras Ma'am, not even bothering to hide the fact that it was a bribe.

'Are there any more people coming?' asked Noor, glancing

at her two fellow experiment subjects and dismissing them out of hand. This was going to be *painful*.

'Yes, one or two.' Saras Ma'am waved the plate of biscuits under Noor's nose. 'You know how it is, these things start slow. Besides, I thought it would be more comfortable with fewer people.'

Another student came in, someone Noor recognized for always sitting in the front of the class and waving her arm around. Divya? No, Diya. Diya had a big, round face and always seemed slightly out of breath. She was also very bossy and had been class monitor for three years running. The kind of person who was always screaming for their team to win, and who designed posters when it was their class's turn to decorate the bulletin boards. Armana was convinced Diya was gay because 'She keeps staring at me!' and once, apparently, when they were both in the girl's loo alone, Diya had touched her shoulder for 'much longer than necessary'. No one had confirmed this, since it had been just Armana and Diya in the loo, but Armana had wrinkled her nose and said, 'Yuck,' and the rest had followed suit, giggling whenever Diya entered the same space as they did, taking turns calling Diya one or the other's girlfriend. Diya seemed completely oblivious to all this, though. She had her own group of friends, two other rather mousy girls, and she had a loud, heckling demeanour when it came to boys.

Diya looked around the room, nodded at Noor and grabbed a biscuit without being asked. The boy smiled shyly at her and Diya responded with a bigger smile. Noor felt a little hurt that she had gotten such a brusque hello but, then again, Diya was probably wary of all the times the Group had giggled when they walked past her.

'Am I late?' asked a voice at the door, and a small boy of about ten came in, his voice still squeaky.

'Not at all, Ankur, come, come,' said Saras Ma'am, and Ankur came in, took his biscuit and sat cross-legged on the floor, his hefty backpack next to him. They all settled in around him, turning expectant faces to Saras Ma'am, who smiled at them.

'I feel like I should make a speech or something,' she said, laughing. 'But no, just . . . Welcome. You're all going through a difficult time in your lives and here are other students who are in the same boat as you are.' She turned to the blackboard. 'Maybe we should start out by giving ourselves some ground rules? Something that all of us come up with so that we can agree. Dem-o-crat-ically. Do you all know what that means?' The younger students shook their heads and Noor tuned out, bored. This was obviously for kids. She didn't belong here. And she was never coming back.

'Noor?' She started back to life at the sound of her name. Saras Ma'am was looking at her, and she wasn't smiling either.

'Yes, Ma'am?'

'I was just saying for the benefit of everyone, we should all make sure we *all* understand all the terms that we use. Like a family. And then I said we should go around the room and introduce ourselves while we give one rule for me to add to the board.'

'Okay,' said Noor. The others looked at her expectantly. 'Oh, is it my turn?'

'That would be nice,' said Saras Ma'am dryly. Diya snorted and rolled her eyes, and Saras Ma'am held up her hand, 'Diya, you'll get your turn.'

'Um, hi, my name is Noor,' said Noor. 'I think a good rule would be that people don't have to talk if they don't want to.'

'How are we going to make any progress then?' shot back Diya, and Noor narrowed her eyes at her. Alone, without her friends surrounding her, she couldn't keep up her front against Diya, who seemed really hostile.

'I just don't think everyone will want to talk *all the time*,' Noor said, and then, channelling Armana, looked at Diya pointedly and said, 'unlike *some* people.'

'Better to talk more than be mute!' said Diya, whose face was getting really red. Noor muttered, 'Wow. Issues.' to herself and looked around for a friendly face to roll her eyes at. None was forthcoming. They all looked at her somewhat goggle-eyed.

'Guys,' said Saras Ma'am, 'that's enough. Let's examine Noor's rule. No one has to talk unless they want to. How many people are in favour of this rule?'

Noor shot her arm up and looked around. The shy-looking girl raised her arm timidly as well. And then, to her surprise, so did the older boy.

'Great, then it's passed.' Saras Ma'am wrote 'No compulsory sharing' on the board and said, 'Who's next?'

Diya said, very loudly, 'My name is Diya and I think anyone who shares what happens here should be suspended from school.' Noor knew this barb was meant for her but she stared steadily ahead.

'Well, that's a good rule, Diya, but I'm sure no one here would break confidentiality,' said Saras Ma'am. 'Even if they did, I can't promise to suspend anyone, but I will put you all on an honour system. Have you heard of doctor-patient confidentiality? It means that a doctor can't reveal anything a patient tells them. In this room, you are *all* patients. You are *all* doctors. The honour system will make this room a safe space. Now tell me,' she glanced at Noor, 'how many of us would like a safe space right now?'

Noor steadily ignored her gaze and returned to fiddling with some loose strings on the carpet which they were all sitting on.

'I would, for *sure*,' said Diya, fervently. 'It's mad at our house. *Mad.*' She gazed at Saras Ma'am adoringly.

'We'll get to that in a second, Diya, but who would like to speak next?'

The girl with the braids raised her hand. 'Hello, my name is Saraswati, and I would like to make a rule that each person has to take turns while talking.' Her expression remained sweet but Noor snickered to herself. Good for Saraswati, sneaking in a bitchy jab!

'That's a great idea, Saraswati! Anyone opposed?' No one was opposed. Saras Ma'am wrote it down on the board and pulled out a conch shell from her bag, telling them it was a speaking conch that they would hold and only the holder would get to speak.

'Cool, a magic conch,' deadpanned the guy right next to Noor. She had almost forgotten about him and glanced at him from the corner of her eye. She didn't have the this-is-cute and this-is-not-cute set of rules in her head that the others seemed to be born with, always telling them which star was currently the hottest, but she thought something about his chin reminded her of Zayn.

The little boy announced his name was Ankur, he was in class six, and his rule was that no one could make fun of him because he was the youngest. There was a gentle, general rush of laughter at that, and he gazed around him, face pink, hair spiky, his hands clenched into fists, ready to take on any bullies.

'Relax, man,' said the guy next to Noor. 'We're all on the same team here.'

'Let's decide that no one makes fun of anyone,' said Saras Ma'am. 'Is that a good rule?' They nodded, Noor drawn along by the rest. After all, if she was on her own, Group-less, and she had no one to make asides to, she may as well participate, she thought.

'*You* haven't said anything,' said Diya piercingly, looking at the boy next to Noor.

'I was just going to,' he said, raising his hands, palms forward in a gesture of surrent. 'I'm Ishaan, I just joined this school two months ago. Um. My rule is that we should *do* something each time we're here instead of only sitting around and talking about our feelings.'

Saras Ma'am raised one eyebrow, Diya inhaled deeply, about to voice her objections, but then Ankur said, 'Yes!' and even Saraswati was smiling—timidly, glancing over at the others to see if she was allowed to smile, but smiling anyway, in a way that made her face look moonlike, with a wedge cut out of it. So Noor was emboldened enough to say, 'That's a *great* idea.' Even if she wasn't coming back, at least she could leave a good legacy for them. Also, anything to be against whatever side Diya was on.

'Well, I had thought of this as a sharing space but maybe you're onto something, Ishaan,' said Saras Ma'am, considering. 'It might be better if we have some activity to look forward to. But . . . hm. What?'

'If I may suggest it,' said Ishaan politely, 'I think Scrabble or, like, any board games might be cool. We can sit around and play and chat, or whatever you'd like?' Noor sort of knew by the tone of his voice that the chatting was what Ishaan was looking forward to *least*. *You and me both*, she thought, and was filled with a warm, happy feeling for having found an ally.

But no, she was totally not coming back for the next session.

'I'll bring Scrabble for our next meeting,' Ishaan was saying. 'You guys will love it.' Diya was still looking sulky, so he asked her specially, 'Have you ever played, Diya?' 'Obvio,' she said. 'Everyone's played. It's *boring*.'

'Well, then you probably lost,' said Ishaan, grinning, and Diya gasped. For a second, Noor thought that there was going to be a fight but then she realized Ishaan had said just the one thing that made it possible to engage with Diya. This hectoring, jibing banter, she understood. She thrived on it, in fact, as you could tell now, one hand in her skirt pocket, the other pushing her hair back from her face, getting louder and louder, 'I COULD BEAT YOU WITH MY HANDS TIED BEHIND MY BACK AND MY BRAIN ON STANDBY!' she was saying, and Ishaan was saying, 'Oh yeah? Prove it!'

Ankur was looking around him, satisfied, and Saraswati said to Noor, politely, 'Didi, you also play Scrabble?'

'Not in years,' said Noor, trying to bury a memory of her parents playing together late at night, after they thought she was asleep, and how she had snuck out to get a glass of water and watched them, her father's face furrowed with concentration, her mother looking placid in her assured victory, and bored, pulling out a piece of knitting and working on that instead. Ammi had spotted her and said, 'Noorie! What are you doing out of bed?' looking very shocked, but secretly delighted at this distraction, and they'd gone off to get Noor a glass of water and maybe some ice cream if there was some in the house, while her father was still staring at the board, forehead creases getting deeper as if the letters would transform into a magical winning word just by sheer will power. And then he'd finally placed his word down with a soft 'Aah' and looked up to see the two of them chatting, and said, 'Arre, Rox, you want to play or what?' as if she had been the one taking forever over the board.

'Well, you can play with us. No one here can probably play very well. Except for Ishaan Bhaiyya.' Saraswati's face went all soft with adoration.

'Winning friends and influencing people already in your first three months at school,' said Noor, snidely, when Ishaan looked up. 'Not bad.'

He was just about to say something, looking a bit surprised at her tone, when Saras Ma'am, who had been tapping on her phone for the past ten minutes, said, 'Okay! That was *grrr-eat* for a first meeting! We'll meet back here on, let's see, what's today? Thursday? Yes, we'll meet back here on Monday. Don't forget to tell your parents you'll need a ride! I'll see you all soon! My door is always open for questions!' And with that, she breezed out, balancing her book bag and empty boxes of biscuits.

Noor prepared to dash too. She picked up her backpack, slung a strap over one shoulder and was about to do the second in a jiffy, when it got tangled in the first and she lost valuable time taking her whole bag off and trying to put it on again.

'How are you getting home?' Ishaan asked, looking down at her with deep concern in his eyes. Oh, as if! She could see through his nice-guy act even if no one else could.

'Auto,' said Noor, curtly.

'Let me drop you, my grandfather sent his car.'

'Um, no thanks. I'm good.'

He looked a bit wounded but then turned and made the same offer to the others. They all had rides, it turned out, except, Diya looked really sad that she couldn't take him up on his ride.

Perhaps just to piss her off, Noor said, 'How do you know where I live anyway?'

'I don't,' he said, smiling a little, 'but it's still no trouble. No one is going to be home at my grandparents' house for a while anyway.' He didn't say, 'And I don't want to be alone' but Noor got it. In unhappiness, at least, the whole room had something in common.

It turned out that they didn't live very far from each other after all—adjoining neighbourhoods. A long walk, but a short drive.

Noor didn't say very much to him in the car but she snuck little glances at him while they were moving along. It was almost sad that she wasn't going back to TOD. However, if he was going to be all annoyingly nice and sweet to everyone, even that ghastly Diya, then he was definitely loser-like material. He didn't *seem* like a loser though.

'Why did you move here?' she asked, just to break the silence.

He looked a bit guarded, then sighed and said, 'I may as well tell you, given the circumstances under which we met.'

She giggled, 'You talk like an uncle.'

He smiled too. 'I watch a lot of really old movies.'

'Anyway.'

'Anyway, so my parents split up and they've been sort of fighting for custody over me, which is really stupid because I'm not a kid, and someone can just ask me. But my mother, she's just using me to get back at my dad. She's moved us here with her parents and there's all this heavy socializing and everything is super fake. I would much rather live with my dad but no one has given me a choice.'

Through this speech, Ishaan looked straight ahead of him, like a soldier, not giving away anything from his expressions, but Noor noticed a twitch in the corner of his mouth, pulling it downwards. She felt really bad for him, and that might explain why she reached out and took his hand in hers. Noor had, literally, never done anything like that before and she was as startled as he seemed to be, almost jerking back but not releasing her hand, which he clasped gratefully.

'What's your story?' he asked her, now turning around

and looking right at her, and she could see his eyes magnified by his glasses, sort of soft brown, almost hazel, long, long eyelashes, pupils that dilated as she looked at them.

'No story,' she said lightly. 'Saras Ma'am just made me come to this meeting. I may not come back. Oh, this is my house.' She tapped the driver on the shoulder to make him stop and dropped Ishaan's hand. 'Bye,' she said casually. 'Thanks for the lift.'

'Can I call you?' he asked, and she shrugged. 'Sure, whatever. I don't use the phone much anyway.'

She wished the Group didn't have such rigid rules about whom they were allowed to associate with and whom they weren't, but so it was. She stood in the foyer of her house and watched him drive by. A nice boy. Their currents had briefly crossed but were unlikely to, again. She ignored the feeling of loss she felt at that, at the idea of never returning to TOD, and went to her room.

'Hey,' said Sanvi on the other end of the phone, 'do you want to spend the night tonight? My brother and I can pick you up. It'll be easier to, like, negotiate with Aryan also then.'

Noor considered her options. There was home with her father, who was working later and later, and the HOC, who was taking over the house with her old age, smelling like mothballs and elderliness, wafts of prayer and incense everywhere. Sanvi's house was a little depressing too—they had too many tube lights and their furniture was all covered with little pink crochet doilies made by both

Sanvi's mother and her brother's wife—but it would be a change. Actually, there really wasn't that much to think about.

'Okay,' said Noor. She'd have to check with her father first, but she was pretty sure he wouldn't care.

'Great!' said Sanvi. 'I'll pick you up in an hour or something. Don't forget your stuff for school.'

Noor hung up and went across the hall to see if her father was home. He was, for a change, lying in bed with his socks on and his shirt off, surfing through the news programmes on TV. 'Dad,' she said, and he looked up startled.

'Hmm? What is it? Have you eaten?'

It was like her father had read a parenting manual where they told you the only thing you needed to know about your kid was the status of their last meal.

She shook her head. 'Is it okay if I go to Sanvi's tonight to spend the night? I'll have dinner there.'

He shook his head as if to clear it and then cleared his throat as well. 'Sanvi's house?'

'Yes,' Noor would not be impatient. It wasn't his fault he didn't know all her friends. They tended to turn into a large twittering mass around fathers, just smiling 'hello' and vanishing. She'd be surprised if any of her friends' dads knew *her* name.

'Sanvi, Dad,' she said. 'You know, sort of short? Lives in Panchsheel Park? She's been here, like, loads of times.'

'Homework?' said her father hopefully. Like 'food', 'homework' was a key word he recognized.

'I'll do it there. We have a maths test we can study for together.'

'Okay,' he said, exhausted from this exchange. 'Tell your grandmother before you leave.'

'What? Why?'

'She'll worry, Noorie, just tell her no? It'll make her happy.'

'I don't want to tell her anything!' said Noor, sticking out her lower lip and catching herself in the act of stamping her foot.

'*Noor.*'

'*Dad.*'

'Just do it. Show some respect. Then you can go.'

Noor ran back to her room to toss some things into a tote bag, checking her timetable for the next day for books, and adding her folded and ironed school uniform on top of the pile. Once, she had forgotten to carry a school shirt, and she had been at Sonum's, who didn't have a spare shirt, so she had been forced to wear a white polo T-shirt with half sleeves and hope no teacher spotted her all day. She rather liked their school uniform—primrose-coloured shirts with bright orange skirts in the summer, and mauve sweaters with striped, grey pants in the winter. For a long time, they had had to wear skirts in the winter too—thicker material, yes, but still skirts—but a few years ago, an enterprising class XII batch signed petitions and called in a designer to show how girls' pants could look modest and, yet, formal at the same time, and got all the parents involved, until the school gave in. She liked her winter pants too—they were meant to be straight fit, but the Group had them made by Armana's tailor and they were slim cigarette pants, the cuffs rolled up.

Noor had once seen an image of sixties' Hollywood actresses, standing around wearing the same pants, oversized sweaters rolled up till the elbow, one of them smoking a cigarette, one of them caressing a poodle and it had all seemed so impossibly glamorous. Sonum had several photos of all of them in uniform, including Noor's favourite—the girls with linked arms, Sanvi bent double with laughter, Natasha saying something at just that moment, Armana bending into Noor and Noor's face turned up, both shining with reflected laughter, and Sonum at the edges, looking anxious but still smiling at the same joke. Noor couldn't remember what they had all found so funny but it was probably something that Sonum had taken a beat longer to get. She had liked that photo so much, she got Sonum to send her a copy, changed it to black and white like the old Hollywood photo and stuck it in a frame in her room. She picked it up now and glanced at it for comfort.

Ammi had loved that photo too, especially because it mirrored one they had from when the girls had just become friends, at ten or nine, all standing in a row around the dining table, about to start singing happy birthday (to Noor, in fact) with the same formation, Sanvi laughing, Natasha pushing her hair back from her face in mid-sentence, Noor turning back from the cake to smile at Armana, who was gazing at her fondly, and Sonum with a birthday hat on her head, looking sideways at them, wondering what was so funny.

Buzz buzz-buzzzz-buzzz went her phone on the table. Sanvi had arrived, probably. Yup, there was a text saying, 'Come down.'

Noor picked up her bag and went down the stairs, pausing to stop at her grandmother's room to tell her she was leaving.

'Where are you going? At this time?' said the HOC.

Noor had planned this. She knew the HOC wouldn't be happy, so she grabbed her key and said, 'Just to a friend's house to study, I'll spend the night, see you tomorrow,' and closed the door firmly behind her so the HOC couldn't argue.

Sanvi was waiting in her brother's car but, surprise-surprise, she was in the driver's seat.

'You're driving?' Noor asked, as she excitedly climbed in.

'Yup!' said Sanvi, 'Bhaiyya finally agreed when I told him we wouldn't go *too* far. And I've been doing pretty well, haven't I?' This to her brother, who was sitting in the front seat, looking at his phone.

'Huh? Yes, not bad,' he said. 'Now get out and let me drive us home.'

'Oh *please*, Bhaiyya, Noor has never seen me drive, can't I drive at least until the next red light?'

'Hi!' said Noor from the back seat. She never knew quite what to say to Sanvi's taciturn older brother Aniket, who already looked adult and careworn, with his paunch and bald spot and wire-rimmed glasses. She was the only only child in the Group but her friends' siblings always felt like her own too: Natasha's younger brother, Armana's younger sister, Sonum's older sister and Sanvi's older brother. Well, not really Aniket, who wasn't much of a sib for Sanvi either. Surprisingly, Aniket was the only thing that disproved the Group's Sanvi-was-adopted theory. He looked exactly like his father, yes, but there was a certain something about his mouth that was reflected in Sanvi's own.

'Hi,' said Aniket back to Noor and then proceeded to gaze at his phone some more.

Noor didn't say anything in the car because Sanvi was really concentrating on her driving, so she hummed quietly to herself in the backseat. Already, her mood was beginning to lift (stupid TOD) and she was able to examine closely her weird interaction with Ishaan. *I mean*, she thought to herself, *holding his HAND? What was THAT all about?* Her stomach twisted in an agony of embarrassment coupled with a really weird feeling of excitement. It had been sort of . . . nice? But he was so unlike the hippy-but-cool Aryan (who was riding the fence in Group opinion) or the super classy, supercool Reansh, who was unequivocally just really good looking. She held her memory of Ishaan up next to Prateek, a possible Group Boyfriend, and decided she liked Ishaan's face better than Prateek's, even though Prateek was friends with Reansh and therefore 'acceptable'. Of course, it totally didn't matter what anyone else thought of Ishaan because she wasn't planning on thinking of Ishaan any time soon. Because look what a mess love got you into.

Nope, no thinking about Ammi either.

They stopped at the stipulated traffic light and Sanvi slid out and into the backseat next to Noor.

'What am I, your driver?' grumbled her brother but drove them anyway.

Sanvi gave Noor's arm a friendly squeeze. 'I'm glad you could come out,' she said. 'We're having channa-kulcha for dinner, your favourite.'

'Me too,' said Noor. 'My grandmother was driving me crazy.'

'Your grandmother is in town?' asked Sanvi, raising an eyebrow. Usually Noor talked about her grandparents visiting a few weeks in advance—her mother's parents were awesome and there was always lots of good food and shopping each time they visited.

'Oh, um, yeah,' said Noor, backpedalling. 'My *dad's* mother. She's *horrible*.'

'Wow, I didn't even know your dad *had* a mother,' said Sanvi, but luckily they were distracted for they had arrived at her home.

'My cousins and aunt and uncle are out of town,' said Sanvi, taking Noor through the back door to her house. 'Which means we have the room *all to ourselves*.' Her eyes glinted at Noor and Noor laughed. At a previous sleepover, they had all had to camp in the living room, speaking in really hushed voices so the gazillions of relatives who lived in Sanvi's house wouldn't hear them. Since then, Armana had said, 'No offence, San-san, but it's just easier to be in one of our homes and I'm sure it's better for you as well.' They had all also spent nights with each other individually, like Noor was doing now (all except Sonum, who lived too far away to be spontaneous), but Natasha had grumbled quietly to Noor about the last night she had spent at Sanvi's. 'That cousin kept *eavesdropping* and we couldn't do *anything*, not even talk, so we finally just gave up and went to sleep.'

Noor dumped her stuff in Sanvi's room (bare walls on her side, her cousin's side full of photos of Shah Rukh Khan) and went out to say hello to her mother. Sanvi's mother was quite nice, even though Sanvi complained about her all the time. She was quiet and liked to cook and looked worried a lot. The sister-in-law was sitting in the dining room as well, helping with dinner.

'Noor beta, it's been a long time,' said Sanvi's mother. 'We're having your favourite for dinner.'

And at this, Noor nearly started to cry. How long had it been since someone knew what her favourite was for dinner? She knew how long: exactly four months and three days.

'Hello Aunty,' she managed. 'I couldn't resist once Sanvi told me.'

'Sit, sit,' said the sister-in-law. 'You're looking thin. Lucky girls, I *toh* gain weight as soon as I even look at food.'

Sanvi's fat nephew toddled in as well just then, and Noor played peekaboo with him, laughing each time he squealed with delight. Sanvi might bitch about her whole family but she did like The Kid, which was what she called him, often buying him little treats when the Group went out shopping.

Finally, after dinner, the two of them were alone again, and Sanvi checked that her door was locked. 'Okay,' she said, her eyes sparkling with excitement. 'Guess what?'

'What?' yawned Noor.

'We are sneaking out at, like, midnight.'

'We're doing *what*?'

'Uff, Noor, don't be such a stick-in-the-mud. I don't know why you're so down in the dumps lately, but this will cheer you up. Aryan is coming to pick us up with a friend and we're going *out*.'

'Out where?'

'Oh, just to his friend's house. I've done this loads of times when the psycho hasn't been here.' Sanvi rolled her eyes at her cousin's empty bed. 'We'll go out through the back and come back in a few hours and no one will know.'

'But we have school tomorrow,' said Noor, timidly.

'Screw school,' said Sanvi, sounding very grown up. 'Noor, really, you've gotta learn to live *some* time. These are supposed to be the best years of our lives!'

'What if we get caught?' asked Noor. Sanvi seemed very sure of herself, but then, Sanvi had never been bothered by consequences.

'We won't get caught, ya. Don't be so boring.'

It seemed to Noor that all the hours between then and midnight stretched long and hard. Sanvi's mother knocking on the door to say goodnight, and Sanvi making her change into her pyjamas so that everything would 'look normal'. Sanvi saying, 'Don't go to sleep, you'll just be sleepy for the whole evening,' while Noor yawned, her eyes filling with water. Sanvi tossing a bunch of tops on the bed and changing into three or four, turning round and round in front of the mirror to see which one looked best on her. 'Here Noor, you wear this,' and Noor was in a strappy, black-lace tank top over her jeans. Sanvi outlining her eyes in kajal and pressing her to wear deep red lipstick. 'I thought this was a chill evening,' Noor said in protest, and Sanvi said, 'Well, you never know.'

It was midnight at last and, true to his word, Aryan called them from around the corner, and Sanvi rose, putting her finger to her lips and smiling. Noor was still tired, still sleepy, still reluctant to leave, but Sanvi was going, and they were friends, so she had to go too.

Aryan was waiting in the car with a friend in the front seat. Noor glanced at him curiously. She had not spent that much time with Aryan—he didn't hang out with them a lot—and he was 'older' which was what made him so mysteriously desirable to Sanvi. Baggy jeans, a tight T-shirt, a lopsided smile, and the way he got out of the car to open the back door for them was . . . nice. She guessed she could see what Sanvi saw in him.

'Hi Noor,' he said, and she said 'Hi' softly and was introduced to his friend in the front seat, who went by the unlikely name of Bagga.

'Where are we going?' asked Sanvi, who had made herself comfortable, flip-flops off and her bare feet stuck through the open window.

'We're just going down to Bagga's house,' said Aryan. 'Nothing fancy.'

Sanvi smiled lazily and Noor realized at that moment exactly how sexy her friend was. It was hard to tell if anyone else was pretty around Armana, but here in this car, where Sanvi was obviously comfortable, she was radiant with escape, her fine, straight hair blew back from her face and her lipsticked mouth stretched into a Mona Lisa smile.

Bagga's house was a little further away than Noor had expected, away from the cocoon of South Delhi, into the narrow alleyways of the West. There, every available free scrap of land was a parking lot, home to shiny, angular cars with bumpers that leered at you, and most proclaimed their owner's pride through stickers on the window. 'JATT AND

HAPPY' or 'PROUD TO BE A PUNJU!'—or a smaller car with a sticker advertising a university abroad. Not a very good college—Noor would have known the name if it was. It would be admissions time for her in another year and pre-everything, in her old life, her parents had taken to discussing her college choices on a bi-weekly basis—but a sticker that said 'Rutgers School of Business' or something, and you'd know, if you didn't know better, that the person who owned the car knew someone studying abroad and that made up for the car being just a Maruti or a smaller Hyundai or something.

Aryan swung into a slot by a public park and Bagga hopped out. 'What'll you guys drink, ya?' he asked Sanvi, who shrugged. 'What do you have?' she asked. Bagga went into a long discourse about the state of his bar (non-existent because of a party his roommate had had) but Noor tuned them both out to look around her.

It wasn't that she had been raised a *snob* or anything, it was just that in her fairly sheltered life, she hadn't seen much beyond what existed in her neighbourhood and other ones around it. Oh sure, once a year, usually in the winter, they'd take a trip on the Metro to Old Delhi, the Metro being half the fun of it, signalling that they were 'off on an adventure', like the Famous Five or something. Her parents had friends in Gurgaon and she visited them, but Gurgaon was like South Delhi, only a bit further away. Her friends all lived in similar versions of homes, differing a bit in décor, or whether or not they had a garden. Even Sonum, who lived somewhere here, lived closer to Central Delhi than they were right now, and she was justified in her home with its acres of manicured lawn and three floors, with a penthouse area for entertaining.

Where she was in West Delhi wasn't a poor neighbourhood but there was something about the houses, built so close together, aggressively competing with each other to look more like a cake, that Noor sensed instinctively that these weren't homes of anyone she could have known. The ugly brown faux brick was a popular choice, resting next to a white monstrosity with a floral cornice that glimmered in the street light. Still, they were all more appealing than the grey, blocky house that Bagga was leading them towards, that had a rusty gate that actually creaked open like it was playing a part. 'Are we being led into an abandoned lunatic asylum?' she whispered to Sanvi, who looked at her a bit blankly and said, 'He lives alone, so he had to take what he could get.' Armana would've laughed. Natasha would have made spooky-sound-effect noises. Noor sighed.

They followed one after the other, up the high staircase, which smelled a bit like sweat and laundry detergent, past a door where a dog hurled itself at the wood and barked from underneath it, past a door decorated with swastikas and little bells and a sticker of Ganesha—and Noor thought, *This is the HOC's dream house,* and *still* couldn't share that bon mot with anyone—past a door that was locked firmly with solid, steel padlocks in three places and finally up to a door on the roof, which Bagga pushed open, panting.

They were standing on a terrace much less depressing than the rest of the house she had traipsed through. Perhaps because it was a terrace, but also perhaps because someone had strung fairy lights across, from pillar to pillar. Bagga? It was hard to imagine him being romantic or fanciful enough to do that, seeing him as he was standing just then, lifting his red T-shirt to scratch at the hairy belly beneath. There was an old-school charpoy facing a steel trunk and a mattress on the floor, on which sat . . . Ishaan.

Noor gave a little start. Next to her, Sanvi, who was holding her by the elbow as if she was afraid Noor would make a run for it, said, 'What? It's not *that* bad, is it?'

'No, I just . . . I know that guy.' Noor gestured with her chin. Ishaan hadn't noticed them yet because they were still huddled by the stairwell and his face was illuminated by the one bare bulb that swung behind him. He was nodding and smiling at Bagga, who said something and clapped him on the back, turning back towards the girls.

'Drinks? Drinks, guys?' asked Bagga, and Sanvi said, 'Sure!' and went off towards the back of the terrace where Noor could see a kitchen. She still stood at the edge, feeling a little shy and very, *very* awkward.

'Would you like a drink?' asked Bagga, looking down at her, and she noticed for the first time how kind his eyes were. His hair hung in shaggy, curly locks around his face and his smile looked tentative, almost. She decided she liked him.

'Um, okay,' she said. 'Do you have any vodka?' Vodka was the only drink she knew to ask for. '*Everyone* has vodka,' Armana had once propounded, '*and* it goes with *everything* and it doesn't make you fat or smelly.'

'Ahhh, man, I wish I had known you guys were coming,' Bagga looked apologetic. 'No vodka, sorry. Nothing but beer.'

Noor hated beer. Hated the way it made her feel full and

bloated and gassy, hated the way it tasted—first bubbles, then bitter, then nothing. She had only tried it twice—once, on a dare at Sonum's house, the other time, when Sanvi had casually brought out a can from her bag and passed it around at one of their sleepovers and Noor had felt too much like a goody-goody to refuse, when even Armana was drinking it, long hair loosely plaited and across one shoulder, like a Budweiser *model* or something.

But she didn't want to be picky either. She knew that boys liked girls who were super girly but also into stuff boys liked. Not that she *cared* or anything, but the Group knew how to be the most charming girls in the room, in *any* room, and the Group's rules usually carried her through uncomfortable social situations. So she nodded at Bagga, who set off to get her one. Noor made to follow him and then saw Ishaan's eyes on her, one hand raised hesitatingly, as if he wasn't quite sure she would say hi to him, in which case he would quickly cover up by pushing back some of his hair or fiddling with his drink.

But Noor was strangely glad to see him. Her heart had risen in a great *THUMP THUMP* when she had first noticed him and had been looking away from him steadily, and now, with them making eye contact, her stomach fluttered with millions of wings. 'Butterflies,' she thought to herself and smiled at him, warmer than she had been meaning to. Too late! Before she could escape to the kitchen and play it cool, he was getting up and walking towards her. Out of his school uniform, he looked older, more adult. He was wearing a grey-and-white striped T-shirt and blue shorts that ended at his knee, and somehow, seeing his calves made

Noor even more shy than she had been before. 'You're so stupid,' she told herself. 'They're only *legs*.' But she could feel the area under her arms grow damper, despite the deodorant, and her palms were sweaty and her legs felt like they couldn't move.

'Heyyyyy,' he said, when he reached her, his eyes gleaming through his glasses. He wore *glasses*. They didn't date boys who wore glasses, unless they were cool glasses, oversized, with black rims for the ironic-hipster effect. Ishaan's were wire-rimmed, *earnest* glasses, glasses through which he was currently blinking at her.

'What are you doing here?' she asked, and it came out urgent and authoritative, not at all cool and casual like she had intended. His face fell a bit and she noticed his mouth did that twitch thing again. She had the absurd image of herself reaching up on tiptoe and putting her mouth on his but she killed it and studied her toes instead. She had painted them last before her mother left, and the faded green was only at the top of her toenails now, showing how long it had been without Ammi.

'Bagga is my cousin,' said Ishaan. 'I didn't have any friends—I mean, I haven't *made* any friends yet, so I thought I'd look him up on Facebook. Then he asked me over. I didn't know there'd be anyone else here tonight.' Bagga came up just then, handing Noor a beer. 'Haywards 5000,' it said in a manly font. It looked and smelled strong, but it was cold and Noor took a sip straight from the bottle, shuddering.

'Not a beer drinker?' asked Ishaan. He was talking right into her ear and she could smell a whiff of the same beer on him. Or was it her breath already? She found she didn't mind the smell on him and took another chug, her tongue pressed against her palate, so she didn't have to taste it.

'Come on, you don't have to drink it,' said Ishaan. 'I'll make you a shandy. Do you like shandies?'

'I haven't had one yet,' said Noor. Normally, she would pretend like she had tried everything, done everything. The boys from her school, the boys she met, also liked girls who were a little world-weary—If you could flip your hair and act blasé, if you could smile a wry little smile, if you could roll your eyes and say, 'Oh God, I'm never trying *that* again.' Sometimes, Noor felt like she was really far behind everyone else in the game of growing up. Her friends had been places, they had eaten things, they had kissed boys, they had probably even had sex. And here she was, lagging behind, nothing checked off on her list of 'Never ever have I evers'. (Except Sonum, and no one wanted to be just like Sonum.)

Ishaan seemed to understand, though. She watched him through her eyelashes as he led the way to the kitchen, poured a little—just a *smidge*—of the beer into a cup, which he sniffed first to see if it was clean, and then he added the Sprite, which rushed glorious and sparkling from its green bottle, covering up the smell of beer and becoming a friendly drink she was happy to accept.

Sanvi and Aryan were still in the kitchen, locked in one of their never-ending fights. Noor was surprised they fought so much, neither of them seemed to have the energy for that much passion in their day-to-day lives. But here they were, Sanvi gesturing with one slender wrist, silver bangles clinking—she hadn't had them on when they'd left the house, Noor would've noticed the noise, so she must have put them on afterwards—her eyebrows drawn together in a frown, Aryan leaning against the counter but not leaning in the louche, loose way he normally did. He was slanting with *tension*, his fists balled up. But then, as abruptly as they had begun, they stopped, the strain draining out of their bodies, and Sanvi reached over—Noor flinched, because she thought Sanvi was going to slap him or something, but she just cupped Aryan's face and Aryan looked down at her with almost-love.

Noor didn't like fighting, she never had and, suddenly, she was reminded of shouting and doors slamming and fights that didn't end with a cupped face, so she grabbed her mug and downed it all in one go and then said in a high, brittle voice to Ishaan, 'Can I have another?'

Ishaan took her mug without comment but there was something about his expression that suggested he knew her motives, and she stepped one step closer to him, one step further away from Sanvi, who was frankly gaping. *Go away*, she thought hard in Sanvi's direction, but Sanvi must not have felt her vibes and was introducing herself to Ishaan.

'Sooo, how do you two know each other?'

'He's in our school,' said Noor, as dully as she could manage, so Sanvi wouldn't ask follow-up questions.

That led to a little do-you-have-this-class and what-section and oh-do-you-know, until Sanvi was satisfied that Ishaan was a new boy and therefore not worth jotting down on her mental map.

'Noor is my *bestie*,' she confided in Ishaan, smiling up at him, and Noor realized she was already a little drunk.

'One of your besties,' said Noor, trying to usher Sanvi out and away.

'*One* of, yeah, we're in the Group together. You must have seen one of our friends, at least. Very tall? Long hair?'

And then Ishaan nodded, because of course he had—who wouldn't notice Armana—and Noor felt small and short and dumpy.

And finally, Sanvi was taken away by her boyfriend, who took her hand and linked fingers with her and smiled at Noor over Sanvi's head, in what Noor realized later was a conspiratorial smile. Like he was doing her a favour.

'Your group is called the Group?' asked Ishaan, when they were alone again. 'Like, with a capital G?' He was actually grinning. Noor crossed her arms. 'Yeah, so?'

'So nothing,' he kept grinning, the fool. 'It's just so mafia of you.'

'It's a stupid name but it stuck,' said Noor. 'We've always been the Group. It's not our fault.'

'No, but you guys call yourselves that too?'

'What is your *point*?' Noor remembered a party trick of Armana's and produced it now. She flipped her hair back from her face and said, 'You're just *jealous*.'

In Armana's cold, very cutting tones, this had left her opponent speechless, but Ishaan just laughed, which made Noor even madder.

'You ever hear that old song from the nineties called "Barbie Girl"? he asked next.

'No,' said Noor, suspecting this was a trap, but all he said was, 'Listen to it sometime.'

'Is that good?' Ishaan asked, gesturing to her shandy,

Noor nodded and he went on, 'So have you all been friends long?'

'About six years.'

'I had a group of friends like that in Bombay,' he said, looking wistful. Or was he looking angry? It was hard to tell through the glasses and through the pleasant haze the shandy was currently giving her vision.

'Is that where you're from?' asked Noor. 'Bombay?' She knew Bombay from her grandparents but with them it always seemed like a very old city. She knew life had to be going on outside the double-glazed windows of their flat, but inside, they all ate large meals and went to sleep by 10 p.m.

'Yeah,' he sipped his beer, 'at least, it's where I grew up. My . . . parents met there. Ma was a Delhi girl first, though.'

'Mine too. I mean, they met there.'

'So in a way, if it weren't for Bombay, we wouldn't have been born.'

They both stood in silence for a bit, contemplating this. Noor was suddenly struck with a sense of vertigo. What if her parents had never met? Who would she be now? No one, she realized. She wouldn't have been anyone if the HOC had had her say from the beginning.

A loud roar of laughter from outside brought her back and when she looked up, Ishaan was considering her intently.

'Do you have any brothers or sisters?' he asked.

'Nope. Just me. You?'

'Same.'

Silence. Ishaan gestured to her glass and Noor finished the last sips and handed it back to him. She heard the fizz of the beer opening, the almost-silent pour of Sprite on top, the clink of ice cubes. Everything was both, sounding very distinct and fading away. 'Maybe I'm drunk,' she thought wildly, holding on to the edge of the counter as though the world might spin and throw her off at any moment.

'I like your name,' he said, stepping a little closer to her. 'It's pretty. Um . . . like you are.'

It's not that people hadn't told her she was pretty before; she had always thought they were just being kind. She knew she wasn't unattractive but she knew she wasn't super-model attractive either. She always wondered why anyone would think she was pretty when there were other more attractive girls always there. Looks were sort of like books: Some books were better than others and you didn't say you liked a less well-written book, did you? Everyone liked the same books, more or less. You could agree that a good book was a good book and so, it was silly to say you thought someone was pretty when there were better examples of the genre, so to speak. But somehow, with Ishaan smiling down at her, she believed him, or at least she *wanted* to believe him. Which was part of what spurred her to repeat what she had done in his car and reach out and take his hand and link her fingers through his. The jolt this time was less than what it had been the first time, perhaps thanks to the fuzziness of the alcohol, but it felt right, his fingers warm and a little dry, easily wrapping themselves around hers like they had been doing this for ages.

Again, they were standing in silence. Noor was so focused on their joined hands that she didn't—*couldn't*—look up at him again. His thumb found her knuckles and gently, he ran it over them. So gently. Sparks trailed off where his fingers were and she felt her stomach knot and unknot, her whole being just there where his hand was. Her cheeks felt hot and she couldn't speak, couldn't even move to lift the mug to her mouth again.

'Hey guys, you okay?' Bagga poked his head into the room and smiled at them, withdrawing when he saw the position they were in. 'Sorry! I didn't mean to interrupt anything!'

'No, it's cool,' said Ishaan, and she wondered how he could still talk without becoming a tongue-tied mess like she felt. He pulled at her hand and they were walking out of the kitchen and through the small bedroom at the back, where there was a large air cooler rumbling and spitting out water. He gestured to the bed and sat down, pulling her down beside him.

'Noor,' he said when they were face to face. She was still unable to look him straight in the eye.

'Hmmm?'

'Do you mind if I . . . ?'

She looked up then and he kissed her.

Later, when she was deconstructing the experience for herself, she couldn't explain how it had begun or how it had ended. Much like with the hand holding, her attention was focused entirely on his mouth—softer than she had imagined, a faint touch of stubble pressed against the side of her mouth—the way he took his hand away from hers and put it at the back of her head, not insistent and clingy but just very gently, like he was guiding her. And her own hand had come up and touched the side of his face. There was no tongue, which always sounded so gross when her friends described it—someone's tongue loose and warm in your mouth . . . *disgusting!* Instead, he took her bottom lip between his own and pulled at it, pushing into her, and she pushed back into him just to see what it felt like and their mouths fell into a rhythm, like she had been *designed* to do this, like it was some dance and she knew all the steps, or a poem and she knew all the words.

It couldn't have been longer than a few seconds, maybe a minute at the most, but when he pulled away, her face actually followed him as if he was a moving car and had stopped abruptly and her body thought they were still going.

'This is crazy,' he said, looking at her. He had taken off his glasses halfway through the kiss, a gesture she hadn't even noticed, but now she saw the soft dents on either side of his nose that they left behind, his slightly mole-ish blinking, and it didn't make her think he was so nerdy or uncool or anything apart from unbearably tender.

'This is *crazeeee*,' he repeated, touching her hair, her face, her mouth, still a little open.

'What is crazy?' she asked, thinking, *Oh my God oh my God oh my God*.

'This,' he gestured at them sitting so close together, her foot out of its ballet flat and on top of his, 'We don't even know each other but it feels like we do.'

She knew what he meant. Somewhere, once, she had read about how when you meet your soulmate, you're pre-programmed to remember them; even if you don't actually know them, some part of your heart, your soul, sits up and says hello and you're drawn to them like you're the kite and they're the wielder of the string, pulling you closer and closer.

He tipped up her face, still pointing downwards. She was feeling so shy and squirmy and *everything* and her whole inner being was being catapulted to strange new places that she found it more calming to study something else— the pattern on the bed sheet, black on orange, weird little squiggles jumping out at her, a print of little stick-figure men and women carrying pots of water and herding cattle. Her hand ran over one nubby bit, picking at it, till the tips of her fingers were almost numb from the friction.

'Hi,' he said, when at last her eyes wandered from the bed sheet up to his face and then away again.

'Hi,' she said, and giggled.

'Have you done that before?'

'No,' she said, and then amended it. 'Not really. There was one guy, Mohit, when we were all twelve—kids—and he kissed me in a movie but I didn't like it.'

'This was nice, though?'

'This was nice,' she managed. And then, her confidence suddenly came back from the mini-vacation it had been taking and she grinned at him, 'Yup. This was *nice*.'

'Good.' His glasses were back on—she was glad because he didn't look so vulnerable—and he was smiling at her. 'I want to tell you *everything*. Like, all my stories, and I want to know all of your stories and I want to talk to you all the time and I want to do *that* again and again and again.'

She understood what he meant so totally that she was nodding along to his words. *Yes*, said her brain to every sentence, *yes, yes, me too, yes* and she said it out loud without even thinking about it. And he kissed her again. This time it was a second kiss, which was perhaps even better than the first, because it was less surprise and more we're-doing-this-again and here's-a-promise-we'll-do-it-some-more.

'Noor?' said Aryan, poking his head through the door. 'Noor! There you are, we have to go.'

'What?' she was dismayed but also brought back to herself. 'What time is it? Why?'

Aryan looked a bit frazzled—he didn't even raise an eyebrow at her and Ishaan, still sitting in such proximity, with such intimacy. He just waved her up and said, 'Hurry up. Sanvi's quite hammered, man, and I just realized it's, like, almost four in the morning and her dad wakes up at, like, five.'

Noor was up and on her feet so fast, she got a bit of a head rush. And Ishaan was saying he'd call her and she realized she hadn't even given him her number but it was too late for that because Sanvi had been throwing up somewhere, apparently (*Oh Sanvi, and I wasn't there*, thought Noor, guiltily, because you don't leave your drunk girlfriend alone at a party) and she was swaying and slurring her words. And together with Aryan, Noor managed to get her down the stairs and into the car.

They didn't say much on the drive home. Sanvi had fallen into a deep, drunk sleep and Aryan was too busy trying to drive as fast as he could to get them back, and Noor's thoughts were mixed between what had happened that evening and what *could* happen when they got home, so when Aryan pulled up somewhere, she was quite shocked to realize they were back already. 'I usually drop her one lane down from hers so no one sees the car,' he said. 'The excuse is usually that she couldn't sleep and so she went to the garden or something. She hasn't had to use it yet, but you might have to say that if anyone catches you.'

'But she smells of booze and cigarettes!' said Noor, alarmed at the idea of hoisting Sanvi all the way down the lane.

'I think she might have some perfume and breath mints in her bag,' said Aryan, and the two of them rummaged in Sanvi's large satchel till they found some body spray which Noor covered her with, from head to toe, till she smelt like a rotting bouquet of flowers, and some *Chutki*, which Aryan poured straight into Sanvi's unresisting mouth.

'Don' wan' go home,' protested Sanvi.

'You've *got* to,' said Noor, worriedly watching the sky turn alarmingly light.

'Don' wan'. *Hate* it,' Sanvi explained. 'Always *hated* it, don' wan' now. Less go Agra.'

Noor rolled her eyes and jumped out of the car but Aryan was saying soothingly, 'Soon baby, soon we'll go to Agra. Just get out of school and out of that house, yeah?'

'Come *on,*' said Noor, opening Sanvi's door and pulling her out of a long, engaged lip-lock with Aryan.

She half-carried, half-dragged Sanvi all the way up the road and through the garden to the back of the house.

The door was still unlatched, the house still quiet.

Noor pulled Sanvi through the house and to the bedroom and, at last, only when she got Sanvi into bed, not bothering about brushing their teeth or changing out of their clothes, she lay down, her heart thumping.

About fifteen minutes later, Sanvi spoke from her side of the room, '*Tol*' you we wouldn't get caught.'

5

So, it went like this with Ammi.

Noor had chanced upon her—'discovered the body', as she would think of it later—sitting in the dark, with a pen and paper in her hand. So quiet had she been that Noor had started when she saw her there.

'Noor!' Ammi said. Her voice had a funny little crack in it. It had been a quiet few days, the fights had mostly stopped and Noor had begun to think everything would go back to normal.

'What are you doing here in the dark?' she asked her mother.

'Oh,' said Ammi, 'I was just thinking.'

And then she got up and turned on the lights and asked Noor what she wanted for dinner and about school, and it was such a regular conversation that Noor couldn't recall the details when she thought of it afterwards, just that the weird feeling she had got when she saw her mother there hadn't been quite exorcised by the seeming normalness of later, but almost.

After dinner, her mother had gone into Noor's room

and sat down on the bed. Noor was already lying there with a book.

'Darling, I love you so very much,' her mother said, and it sounded so much like a preamble, an introduction to what was to come, that Noor braced herself, even though she didn't know what she was bracing herself for.

A man Ammi had known when they were both teenagers. 'Sunny Uncle', her mother called him. Sunny Uncle had re-entered her life six months ago and now he was going to bear her away. Noor felt her chin tremble, her heart beat faster as her mother confessed to all of this. 'You must know that Dad and I have been fighting so much lately?' her mother pleaded, trying to catch Noor's eye. But Noor looked resolutely away.

Everything bad happened faster than anything good, in Noor's opinion. When you were waiting for a summer holiday or your birthday, the days stretched on. When your mother left your father and you, without so much as a backward glance, it was all wrapped up in a week. Once Ammi told her about Sunny Uncle, she seemed to be in a hurry to reveal everything about him: Sunny Uncle had never married because he had always loved her. Ammi and he had broken up in their very early twenties over a disagreement and had never spoken again. He had emailed her six months ago, wanting to reconnect, and they had realized they still loved each other. Sunny Uncle was a professor; he was teaching in a university in America but he was going to relocate to Paris, where Ammi would move too. He was in Delhi and Ammi was going to stay at his hotel.

'Did you ever love Dad?' asked Noor in a passion, one day.

'Of course I did! I will always love your father,' said Ammi, and Noor hated her for looking so righteous, as if she had never done anything wrong. 'But what I feel for Sunny is different. I realized that when I met him, Noor.'

And when she left, just packing a small suitcase, she looked at Noor and said, 'You want me to be happy, don't you, Noorie?'

Did she want her mother to be happy? The correct answer was yes. But Noor wasn't sure. Why couldn't Ammi just play along, just squeeze herself into this life? It wasn't *such* a bad life after all. It was the only life Noor had known. Mothers weren't allowed to change their lives, at least, not while their most important role was being Mother. It might have been selfish to think that way but Ammi was the *most* selfish, leaving them behind, her broken father and her—'If you stay in Delhi you can finish school with no disruptions and come join us when you're done,' Ammi had said, but obviously, she was being left behind so the two of them could be alone. Would her mother have *sex* with this man? Noor couldn't even think of it, and when she did, she wanted to throw up. *Obviously*, they would have sex, that's why Ammi left them. Obviously, this sex was more important than the family Ammi had created.

'*I never asked to be born,*' thought Noor bitterly. '*And I will never, ever fall in love.*'

Love. All it caused was trouble, and the incredibly stupid thing about it was that everyone *knew* that love = Trouble-with-a-capital-T. Poets knew it and bands knew it and book writers knew it. And the movies wouldn't be movies without the whole love-sucks-but-in-the-end-everything-is-great storyline. What Noor didn't get was why people didn't just avoid that part of the story arc and save themselves so much trouble. It didn't add anything to your life. Like, think of Armana's ex-boyfriend, Anirudh. He had been head over heels for Armana and where had that led? To Armana being able to break his heart, kicking it around like a pebble. If he hadn't fallen for her, he could have saved himself all that time weeping over her and done something useful. Noor wasn't sure yet, what she wanted to do with the rest of her life but it would be incredibly rewarding and would require all of her mind and so, not falling in love fit in perfectly.

Also, love had sort of been her father's downfall. Never the most chatty man, in the months following Ammi's absence, before the HOC had moved in, he had become pretty much a recluse. He nodded at her briefly when they passed in the hall; sometimes, they both warmed up their dinner at the same time and then flitted away, she to her room and he to his. Once, in an excruciatingly embarrassing moment, he had clutched her head to his chest and said in a broken voice, 'You're all I have now, *all!*' and Noor had stood there, waiting to be released.

That's the one thing she had to say for the HOC. Noor studied her now, over her roti and bhindi. (Bye bye, meat in the house! Bye bye, the friendly smell of her father's scotch!) The HOC had provided Dad with a distraction, and she was always *on* him, fluttering over him when he ate, passing him the first of the hot rotis—even, like, right now, when Dad didn't need anything—just, like, *gazing* at him like some devoted spaniel. Dad looked up then, and caught Noor's eye and smiled at her and Noor noticed a lightness in his smile that had been gone for so long. If her mother was away and cavorting with her lover, then maybe her dad could have his mum nearby for sustenance or something.

And I'll just do it alone, she thought to herself bravely. She wasn't sure why she hadn't told her friends yet. Actually, that's not true. She had a fairly good idea. They saw her mum one way: cool Rox, Roxy Khala, and here she was, this (*whore*, Noor's brain whispered) fallen woman, this mother who had defied motherhood and run away to Paris. Then, after having digested this information, always probably thinking *slut* in their own minds, they'd try to jolly her out of it. 'Paris! How exciting!' Natasha would say, and Armana would talk about a few boutiques that Noor absolutely *must* go to when she visited and Sanvi would say something like, 'I wish *my* mother would leave my father so I could leave with her' and Sonum would say something gauche and horribly naive like, 'Is Sunny Uncle going to be, like, your *dad* now?' and she would want to stab a fork into her own eye because they wouldn't *get* it. *No* one would get it.

She had come awfully close to telling them everything—Ishaan, her runaway mother, her horrible grandmother—at the Group party, or at least at the sleepover after that. But, in the end, the evening turned out to be about Sanvi, who was horribly drunk again and squatting over the loo, puking, and Armana looking disgusted and saying, 'I think she's an alcoholic' and Natasha holding Sanvi's hair back but looking dreamy eyed because Prateek had been invited and he had spent the whole evening looking at her and talking to her, and Sonum saying, 'Guys, have you seen my phone charger?

It was right here' and then having a meltdown because her charger was lost—how would her parents contact her—until Armana reminded her that her parents had all their numbers too. And Sonum calmed down so fast, it was painfully obvious that the whole thing had just been a ploy for attention.

The phone rang and the HOC looked irritated. 'Who calls so late at night?' she grumbled, and Noor said, 'I'll get it' and was out of her chair and bounding across the house for the landline (barely used, but still useful) before she had to sit through any more of the HOC's dinnertime conversation. (Her knees hurt, her hip hurt, today she had such a major headache that even the balm she had put on it didn't work, why did God have to take away her husband?)

'Hello?' said Noor into the phone. She was almost convinced it was going to be her mother and so when the voice at the other end said 'Hello?' back, she was disappointed so deeply, she couldn't speak for a second.

'Is that Noor? It's Ishaan.'

Ishaan! Noor cradled the cordless phone receiver between her ear and her shoulder and slid down the wall till she was squatting against it, her weight supported by her thighs. This posture hurt a bit but helped her focus.

'Hi Ishaan,' she said, waiting.

'I didn't have your cell number, so I asked around for your landline.'

'Okay.'

'So, um, how are you?'

'I'm good. We were just having dinner.'

'Oh, sorry! Do you have to go?'

'No,' said Noor, shifting so she was sitting on the floor instead of squatting. It was dark in the landing where the phone was but she felt comforted by the dark, like he couldn't see her face, which he couldn't anyway. It was silly, but there it was.

'How was your weekend?' asked Ishaan. She thought about his face for a second and then immediately, her thoughts flashed to kissing him, kissing him *hard*, and blood rushed to her face. Her stomach did that funny squirmy thing again. When she didn't answer, he asked her again and his voice had a smile in it.

'It was . . . good,' Noor said. 'We had a party. Spent today hanging out just watching some TV. Finishing my homework. You know.' Wow, she sounded super lame.

'I was at Bagga's again yesterday,' said Ishaan, as if they were having a perfectly normal conversation instead of her answering him in her short, staccato sentences, leaving him no room to reply.

'That's cool,' said Noor, and then, because she didn't want the conversation to end, 'it must be nice to have a friend here.'

'Well, he's family, so I don't know how much of that is obligation,' Ishaan sighed heavily. 'But yeah, at least it's something to do. My grandparents had this dinner party yesterday and I was glad to get out of the house.'

'I know what you mean.'

The phone buzzed with static from their silence and Noor decided to end the conversation even though she didn't want to.

'I should go,' she said.

'Yeah, cool, cool.' Ishaan waited, and then, 'Are you going to come to TOD tomorrow?'

'TOD is such a stupid name,' Noor said, and was rewarded by a huff of his laughter.

'I know, it's so cheesy. But will you come? I'm bringing the Scrabble.'

Noor considered. To TOD or not to TOD? To go would mean to hang out with a bunch of really enthu kids and bossy Diya, but she'd see Ishaan again, which would be brilliant. Perhaps she could even name the feelings he gave her . . . did she *like*-like him? Was this just PMS behaviour? To not go would mean coming home to the HOC and she hated coming home. It seemed a pretty easy choice.

'Okay,' she said. 'I guess I'll come.'

'Oh, that's awesome!' he said. 'I thought maybe after, we could go get ice cream or something? I'll drop you home.'

'*Like a date?*' thought Noor, but, 'Sure,' she said, sounding a lot calmer than she felt.

'Great! See you tomorrow. Bring your Scrabble A game.'

And he was gone, with a casual 'bye' and a click, not even waiting for her to whisper a breathy 'later' like she had been practising in the mirror.

Talking to Natasha online later:

    noorkhanrai: hey
    nutsforyou: hey
    noorkhanrai: question
    nutsforyou: shoot

Was Natasha still being a little weird? Noor found it hard to tell. Over the past few months, even before they had had that *strange* disagreement, she had felt Natasha pulling away from her, becoming this other person. Natasha and she had met first, out of the whole group, and had consistently been in the same section since they were little kids. The others were in and out but Noor and Natasha understood that every year they'd be sitting next to each other and exchanging homework information and getting each other's days in a way the others couldn't.

The whole Group was bffs, besties for *lyf*! But Natasha was her Special in a way the others weren't. In fact, the other three didn't even have a Special. They were close but not in the way Natasha and Noor were, and Armana, who wanted everything, had been making solo plans with Natasha for the last few months, just about the time she had started to be—if not cold—*colder* to Noor than she had been before. Now, Noor would emerge from class to find that Natasha had already overshot her and was standing with Armana, laughing about something. Or, Natasha would look at her phone in the middle of class and giggle and Noor would whisper, 'What?' and Natasha would be like, 'Oh, nothing, just Armana being a goof.'

In fact, now Noor was the unmoored one, floating between Sonum and Sanvi, and she didn't even *like* Sonum all that much. And there was no one to *get* her, to figure out what she meant just by shrugging her shoulders, because those two now were Armana and Natasha. However, the two of them together looked more *right* than Noor and

Natasha ever had. Armana was the prettiest girl in school and Natasha was the coolest, and watching their heads together—long loose braid against pink highlights, perfect mouth rising in a smile to meet a lopsided dimple—they seemed *matched*. Last week, Noor had had to duck into the girl's bathroom to keep from crying when she saw the two of them get out of Armana's car together, Armana pulling on her school shirt over a very familiar Ministry of Sound tank top that was Natasha's favourite.

noorkhanrai: btw, are we good? We haven't spoken much lately.
nutsforyou: god, noor, don't be so needy.
noorkhanrai: haha
noorkhanrai: you're right.
noorkhanrai: anyway, so i think i have a date tomorrow
nutsforyou: omg
noorkhanrai: i know right? it just HAPPENED
nutsforyou: you HAVE to check out armana's latest instagram post! haha she's so crazy
noorkhanrai: um
noorkhanrai: ok
nutsforyou: i gtg nkr, see you tomorrow xxx

And nutsforyou was logged out. Actually, there was still a little green dot near her name but Noor knew if she sent her any messages, Natasha would now ignore them.

noorkhanrai: hi
sansansanvi: yo chica

noorkhanrai: haha, hows it going

sansansanvi: terribly. psycho brat cousin has just returned

noorkhanrai: ugh poor you

sansansanvi: i'm sitting in our room pretending to do homework

noorkhanrai: while ive got you, i think i have a date tomorrow

sansansanvi: :O

sansansanvi: WHO

sansansanvi: TELL ME EVERYTHING

noorkhanrai: um, remember that guy we met at the party

noorkhanrai: from school

noorkhanrai: the new guy

noorkhanrai: ishaan

sansansanvi: oh yeah remember him vaguely. tall guy, right?

sansansanvi: i could tell you guys had some serious VIBAGE

noorkhanrai: shut up!

sansansanvi: its true! haha even aryan said

sansansanvi: gotta tell him he was right

noorkhanrai: well, we're going out to have ice cream or something tomorrow after school

sansansanvi: aw, an ice-cream date!

noorkhanrai: don't be condescending. some of us haven't had boyfriends since we were born

sansansanvi: only joking, noooooor. how did you meet him anyway?

noorkhanrai: um, just, you know, around

sansansanvi: this all sounds very mysterious and i look forward to hearing more

sansansanvi: sadly ive got to jet. family shit. remind me to tell you how to kiss tomorrow

noorkhanrai: actually

noorkhanrai: we've already kissed

'Let's talk about why we're all here,' said Saras Ma'am, sitting on the table and swinging her legs.

'To play Scrabble!' said Ankur, and burst into very juvenile giggles. It was clear that Saraswati, sitting next to him, thought so too and she gave him a *look* and rolled her eyes in the universal language of 'ugh, boys'.

'To learn how to talk about our *feelings*,' said Diya, looking smug when Saras Ma'am nodded.

'To get away,' said Ishaan, whom Noor still couldn't look directly at. He shot her a little smile and she felt panicky. What if he *tried* too hard? What if she got bored of him and hurt his feelings?

'What about you, Noor?' asked Saras Ma'am. 'Why are you here?'

All eyes on her, and Noor, who generally didn't mind speaking up in class ('a lively participant,' one of her report cards had said), felt her face get hot. 'Um. What the others said, I guess?'

'Hmm,' said Saras Ma'am, and Noor looked innocently back. *You can force me to be here and to participate but you can't force me to share my feelings*, she thought. Her teacher blinked first and looked away from Noor to the rest of them.

'This is our second meeting and I'm happy to see you all returned for it. Attendance is not mandatory, though I might have urged you to come for the first.' *Ooh, low blow, Saras Ma'am.* Noor studied her through her eyelashes but she looked as innocent as Noor had just a few moments ago.

'But now you're all here again and I want you to ask yourselves: why am I here? What is my aim?' Saras Ma'am looked at all of them in turn, an Armana trick that got them all to pay attention to her. 'Even if it is just for the games and the food.' Here she smiled, and they all realized her lecture was over and with a big whoop, Ankur ran over to the day's spread (mushroom patties, jam biscuits).

They must really starve that kid at home, Noor thought to herself idly, when Ishaan appeared next to her and murmured, 'He reminds me of my dog, Rufus, when he was a puppy. No matter how much we fed him, he always wanted more.' Noor laughed and turned her head away from him because, suddenly, she smelled a very light whiff of the cologne he had been wearing the other night, mixed with detergent and general human smells. *Nice* human smells, though. Clean sweat. Slight soap. Talcum powder. She couldn't identify it but if you blindfolded her with a bottle full of him, she'd be able to tell you exactly who it was and exactly how it made her feel. Hot and dizzy.

They sat down to Scrabble and, alongside the game, Saras Ma'am led a general discussion on words and how they made them feel. 'Conflict words', she called them. 'What words inspire the *most* emotion in you right now?' she asked.

'Tree,' said Diya, unexpectedly. They all looked at her

and she crossed her arms over her chest. 'What? There's this *damn* tree—'

'Language,' said Saras Ma'am.

'Sorry,' said Diya, continuing. 'Anyway, there's this old champa tree that's been in our garden since my grandparents got married. My grandfather actually planted it the day my grandmother came to his home as a new bride. And my father never really cared about the garden—it's my mother's pride and joy. She spends all her time out there now, especially since they've been fighting. But now, my dad wants to uproot the tree and put it in a pot and take it to his new house, and my mother has been crying over that da—*stupid* tree, like it's more important to her than me and my brother.'

Out of breath, Diya stopped talking. 'Does your father's new home have space for you two?' asked Saras Ma'am, gently.

'*No*! That's just it! He went and got himself this one bedroom with a little balcony and that's where this tree will live, and all they're doing is fighting over the tree and . . .'

'And you feel like no one cares about you?' suggested Saras Ma'am.

Diya burst into tears, surprising them all. She didn't so much *burst* as overflow—her face went very pink and her eyes just welled up and spilled on her face, her rather large mouth pointed downwards and her forehead squinched up. Noor felt uncomfortable watching her and was glad she was on the other end of the Scrabble circle and wouldn't have to comfort her, as the others were doing—Saraswati with one small hand on Diya's large shoulder, Ankur making worried noises, even Ishaan was rubbing his hand in circles on Diya's back, which made Noor feel funny. She wasn't *jealous*. It was just that Diya was getting all the attention. She tossed her head and swished her ponytail for confidence. It helped.

After Diya was done sniffling, Saras Ma'am said they had time for one more conflict word if anyone else would like to share. Diya looked at them all with pleading eyes and you could tell that she didn't want to be the only one with a weird meltdown that afternoon.

'Bombay,' said Ishaan, finally, when no one else rose to the bait. The fun mood Scrabble had put them in was over, and Noor felt vaguely resentful. It had been the first time her chest hadn't tightened in *weeks*.

'Go on,' said Saras Ma'am.

'It's not a conflict word but it makes me feel sad each time I think about it. Every time I hear 'Bombay', even in the news, I think of home and the way it smells and the sea and my friends and everything, and it's like being homesick for something but you don't know how to go back to it. Some things about Delhi are *great*,' here he looked at Noor, 'but I can't help thinking that my heart is still there somehow.'

There was a solemn pause when he finished, which Saras Ma'am broke. 'We've done great work here, guys. See you Wednesday. If you'd like to play a game of Scrabble again, bring it along.'

They were all getting ready to leave, when Ankur said suddenly, 'Oh! Oh! I almost forgot! I have a nouncement!'

'It's *announcement*,' said Diya, who seemed to have

recovered fully from her crying jag and looked, if possible, even more smug than before.

'No,' said Ankur patiently, 'it's only 'an' if the word begins with a vowel. A *nouncement*.'

Noor giggled and Ishaan said, 'Go on then, champ.'

'It's my birthday on Friday. I would like to invite you all to my birthday party. My mother said I should call all my new friends. I printed out invitations.' Here, he reached into his backpack and pulled out a stack of sheets, which smelled warm and looked like they had seen better days.

Noor took the one he handed her. A kid's birthday party? The Group would never let her hear the end of it. But she liked Ankur, with his spiky hedgehog hair and his sudden laugh and his way of barreling straight into things. He was sort of like a little brother. She realized she had already made up her mind. Both, that she would go and that she wouldn't tell any of her friends about it.

'If that's all,' said Saras Ma'am, 'you guys need to split. We're here beyond hours and I have to lock up and give the caretaker the key.'

'Split is a much better name for us than TOD,' said Ishaan. 'That's why we're all here. Because our families have split.'

'And we're kind of split ourselves,' said Noor, surprising herself by participating. The look of approval Ishaan gave her made her feel warm inside, though.

'And this is like a way of talking about our split lives,' said Diya, not wanting to be left out.

'I like the way it sounds,' said Saraswati. 'Much nicer than *die-vorced*.'

'Okay, okay, Split Gang, I get the message,' laughed Saras Ma'am. 'Forgive your old teacher for not having an imagination. Now go on, leave!'

*

Alone in the car with Ishaan, Noor had another attack of not being able to look at him, but she gave herself a stern talking to when he excused himself to use the loo before they left.

'This is just *silly*, Noor Khan Rai,' she said to herself. 'How on earth do you plan on having a boyfriend if you can't even look him in the face?'

So she tackled it bit by bit. When Ishaan came back and gave the driver directions, she turned to face him and focused her gaze on his nose. She stared so long and so pointedly at it that he first brushed the tip with his finger and then gave a puzzled laugh. 'Is there something on my nose? Oh God, there's a booger, right? Here I am, trying so hard to impress you and I have snot on my face.'

'No!' said Noor, laughing delightedly. 'I was just . . . There's nothing on your nose.'

'How can I believe you when all you're doing is staring at it? Is it weird? Do I have a strangely shaped nose?'

Now she would *have* to tell him, or risk him being body-shamed for his nose (which was rather nice, all things considered).

'I was feeling too shy to make eye contact,' she said, and heaved a huge sigh of relief. Wow, it felt good to get that off her chest.

Ishaan looked baffled. 'Um . . . is that a Delhi thing?'

Noor laughed until her eyes welled up with tears. It felt so good to dissolve into mirth. *People don't usually make me laugh so much*, she thought, *usually, when I think of the Group, I think of us laughing, but we're not really LAUGHING. Not like this.*

'It's not a *Delhi thing*,' she managed finally.

Ishaan smiled at her, 'Go on staring at my nose as much as you like, if it's such a joke,' he said. 'I like your laugh.'

'Yeah?' Noor had never given much thought to her laugh—it certainly wasn't pealing bells or tinkling stream or whatever the books made you think it was, always some euphemism that sounded more like it was describing pee than anything else—it was just a normal laugh, half ha ha, half sharp breaths through the nose.

'Yeah. You're cute when you laugh.' Ishaan leaned over and Noor caught her breath, all amusement gone. But all he did was pinch the tip of her nose. 'Your eyes get all lit up. I never thought that was a real thing, but you looked happy. Happier than you've looked since I first met you.'

Noor looked into his eyes, really looked, for the first time since she had seen him that day, and was surprised to find how easy it was.

'Wasn't so hard, right?' he said, half smiling, and she shook her head and he leaned over and at that very interesting moment, the driver stopped and Ishaan raised his head.

'Oh look, we're here!' he said, and opened the car door.

Noor sat still for a second, just gathering her thoughts and trying not to look disappointed. Ishaan came round her side of the car, opened the door for her and extended his hand. 'My lady.'

He is such a goofball, thought Noor fondly, and put her hand in his. 'Kind sir,' she said.

They were facing a large glass window that looked like it was the front of a new cool café or something. Noor noticed there was a huge display case at one end and people milling about with cups and cones. 'Naturals' said the sign above her head. She had heard of this—but where?

'Bombay's finest, right here in Delhi,' said Ishaan, still holding her hand and leading them through the door. Oh right. Her grandparents sometimes had tubs full of Naturals ice cream in their freezer. Tender coconut (yuck) for Ammi and strawberry for Noor.

Ammi doesn't even know I am on a date right now. That thought was so alien to Noor that she stopped to contemplate it. Ammi, who had once known every single little detail of Noor's life, who was her closest confidante ('I can talk to *my* mother about *everything*,' she had said tauntingly to her friends), who was the one who had explained periods and boys and sex and how you know when you're ready to be kissed. ('Sadly, my Noorie, you usually only know you're ready right *after* you've done something. Before, you can trick yourself into thinking something is so cool or that it's so right for you to do. But immediately after—or during, if the during is long enough—that's when your gut talks to you and says, "I don't like this! Stop!" and by then it's too late, so you should put it off for as long as possible.')

That's all you know, Ammi, said Noor in her head, *I was SO ready. You don't know ANYTHING.*

'Hey.' A soft touch on her shoulder brought her back to

the present—loud noises around her, Ishaan looking down at her, one eyebrow raised. 'You okay?'

'Uh huh,' said Noor, 'Sorry, I was just somewhere else for a second.'

'You looked it. You completely zoned out of my two-hour lecture on why this is the best ice cream in the world.'

Her heart was a balloon again. She grinned at him. 'Did your lecture have PowerPoint? I can only pay attention if there are pretty pictures for me to look at.'

'Such a child of the Instagram age.' He sighed theatrically. 'No use for good old-fashioned learning.'

'I only read stuff in 140 characters,' she agreed sadly.

'Well, at least this class has a practical exam.'

'It does?'

'It does. Pay attention, class. For fifty thousand marks on your next grade. Which is the best flavour of Naturals Ice Cream?'

'Ooh, I know, I know!'

Ishaan looked at her and then around her. 'I'm sorry, are you trying to participate in class? I only listen to students who raise their hands.'

Noor giggled and raised her hand a little bit.

'That won't do, cadet!'

'Oh, we're in the army now?'

He leaned forward and wiggled his eyebrows. 'Baby, we're always in the army.'

'You're so silly!' said Noor, charmed.

'My silliness has no bearing on the fact that you still haven't raised your hand, Ms Rai.'

'I beg your pardon, it's *Khan* Rai. Being a woman of the

twenty-first century and not defined by patriarchy and all.'

'Ooooh, big *words*,' he said, pretending to stagger back. 'Big, huge words! How will a man like me *ever* understand?'

'Well, maybe if you paid more attention in class?' suggested Noor. 'As I was saying, strawberry is obviously the best flavour. I win and now I'm the teacher. Questions?'

'Yes: strawberry is decidedly *not* the best flavour.'

'Um, that's not a question, it's a *statement*, and also, um, *false*.'

'Strawberry is fine, I grant you, for this pink thing that you 'women of the twenty-first century' seem to like so much. But the clear winner is coffee with walnut.'

'You know nothing, Jon Snow!' said Noor, quoting from a favourite contraband TV show she downloaded and watched in private.

To her pleasure, he got the reference and smiled an acknowledgement at her before quoting from the same show as he linked their fingers together and pulled her towards the display. 'The day is bright and full of ice cream.'

Later, as they were sharing two cups (coffee *and* strawberry as a safe compromise), he said, 'Are you ever going to talk about it?'

'Am I ever going to talk about what?' asked Noor, while privately thinking that the coffee walnut was far superior to the strawberry but she wasn't going to ever admit it.

'About your parents?'

Noor shifted in her chair. 'Let's leave all that split stuff at the Split Club.'

'You know, you'd feel better if you *did* talk about it, though.'

'There's nothing to say,' she said, shrugging. 'It's a thing. I'm dealing. End of story.'

'I don't know if you just don't want to talk about your stuff or don't want to talk about divorce at all.'

'What do you mean?'

'I mean, I'd like to tell you things. I think you'd get it and it would make me feel better. But if you're *uncomfortable* with the whole topic, then I'll drop it.'

'No, tell me,' said Noor, partly because she felt it was expected of her and partly because she wanted to know everything about him. *Everything.* From how he had got his name to the songs he loved to what toothpaste he used. In a weird way, it sort of felt like they were old friends who had been hanging out forever. Noor felt so comfortable with him, she didn't even care that she had managed to spill some coffee ice cream on her yellow shirt, a stain that would probably not come off at all.

'I feel like we've known each other for a really long time,' said Ishaan just then and Noor started. 'I was *just* thinking that!' she said, and he said, 'Just proves it then,' and they both smiled at each other and Ishaan reached out to tuck a bit of her hair behind her ear.

Is he EVER going to kiss me again? thought Noor. *I mean, he was pretty okay with kissing me that night, but that could have been the booze as well. Although, do I want to be kissed in this crowded place with so many people watching?* She looked up and found that the top floor of the ice-cream parlour was full of young couples, most with their heads close to each other, murmuring. The only person paying her any attention at all was a little girl with two pigtails, who was gazing at her so hard, she was dripping her chocolate ice cream all over the front of her pink frock.

'There was a Naturals down the road from my house in Bombay,' said Ishaan, and Noor understood that this wasn't a kissing moment. It was a let-me-tell-you-a-story moment. She liked the way he began his stories, like they were actual stories, like he was the hero in an indie movie and was meant to be lit by soft light, his narrative accompanied by the strumming of a guitar.

'I shouldn't say *was*, there probably still is a Naturals. It's sort of hard to think of it without me there, you know? Like the whole city is on pause waiting for me to get back or something. Anyway, so when I was a kid, Sunday morning was when my parents sent me out to get ice cream for after lunch. I was this really enthu kid, up by dawn and tearing around the house till someone woke up to amuse me. I think that's why they never had any other kids because they thought, man, if we have to deal with *two* of *him* we'll never get any sleep again.

'But when we got our Sunday-ice-cream ritual down, my dad would leave the money on the table by the door on Saturday night and Sunday morning I would wake up and potter around for a bit—I'd wake up at like six? And the shop only opened by nine-thirty if you were *lucky*. Usually ten. So I'd have four hours to amuse myself and, often, this involved banging on my parents door at eight when I was bored, and my dad would tell me to fuck off and go watch TV through the closed door—oh no, don't look shocked, he didn't *really* say fuck, he said, 'Go use your inner resources I'm paying good money for you to develop'—and I'd watch

TV or read a book or something, getting myself a snack. Sunday was the best day because I could eat chips and Coke for breakfast and my mother wouldn't be awake to stop me. And when I was a little older, I kind of liked having the house to myself in the morning, and I'd go get the ice cream and by the time I came back, my parents' room was open and my mother would be in this silk bathrobe of hers, making coffee, and they'd finally talk to me but they'd keep looking at each other and smiling. And finally, I figured out that Sunday morning was when they had sex.'

Noor opened her mouth and then closed it. Of course, she thought about sex. She thought about sex as much as any average teenager did (which was a lot, according to the magazines), but she never thought of her *parents* having sex. Gross! Parents weren't meant to be physical with each other, that was only for people without kids. But she tried to remember when the last time was that her parents were openly affectionate, and it had been a very long time ago. Her mother liked to pass her father and drop a kiss on top of his head. Sometimes, long ago, her dad would grab her mother and she'd say, 'Stop! I have loads of work to do!' and he'd say, 'I'll give you loads of work to do!' and she'd either slap his hand away, her eyes bright, or she'd follow him into the bedroom and their door would close and lock firmly, and Noor would continue whatever she was doing, humming, because—she now realized—her parents were happy.

'Weird, huh, to think of your parents doing it?' asked Ishaan, wryly. 'When I finally figured it out, I got kind of *angry* with them, you know, like, how dare you have alone time without me—the curse of the only child—but by then, they had stopped anyway.' He stretched his hands over his head and glanced out of the window. The light had changed from bright to the soft filter of evening. 'Wow, look at the time! I should get you home.' He stood up and reached for her paper cup so he could put it in the bin.

'I know what you mean,' said Noor, but so softly that no one heard her, not even she herself.

6

The next morning, as Noor was dressing for school, her father knocked on her door and poked his head in.

'Ah, listen, Noor, your grandmother isn't well.'

Noor continued sliding a sock up her foot. Okay, so her grandmother wasn't well. Noor was still going to miss the bus if she didn't leave in exactly seven minutes.

'And I have a meeting,' continued her father.

Noor had a very bad feeling about where this conversation was going. She stopped—one sock on, one sock off—and looked her father straight in the eye. He had the grace to look a little embarrassed.

'Well, I was just thinking, what if you stayed home and looked after her today?'

'Me?'

'I have no one else to call,' Dad spread out his hands in a helpless gesture. 'I would have asked Radha Didi but she's not answering her phone this morning. Do you have anything big at school today? Any tests?'

'No, but . . .' Noor considered. A day off was always welcome. But she wasn't sure she'd be a good nurse.

'What's wrong with her?' she asked, just to clarify.

'Oh, nothing, nothing.' Her father looked relieved. 'Just a mild fever, some aches and pains. You won't even have to sit with her all day, just check in once or twice. Make her some tea. Listen to her when she says something. You know what I mean.'

'Fine,' said Noor. Secretly, she was rather pleased at the prospect of a holiday, but best not to let the grown-ups know how you felt about things in case they used it against you.

When she was very young and fell sick, her mother used to skip work too, and Noor would lie in bed and nap, waking up to her home at an unfamiliar time—11 a.m. on a Monday, say—and all the sights and sounds would be different. There wouldn't be the weekend bustle, just the quiet sound of the music system on in another room. Then, her mother would come in and give her some milky tea and take her temperature. 'Poor baby,' her mother would say, resting her cool palm against Noor's forehead. In that moment, Ammi seemed larger than she was, a sort of conqueror, so capable in all that she did, from shaking out the Crocin packet to give Noor one, to being so confident that she would get well in a specified number of hours. And the best part about staying home, sick, was the recovery—when Noor felt fine, but was still deemed too weak to go to school—then she would sit around in her pyjamas all day, in bed, while her mother brought her books and fruit, and sometimes hummed while folding Noor's clothes. She felt so safe, so taken care of—soppy, mushy baby food, like khichdi, brought up to her bed and her mother wheeling in her large armchair so she could work while Noor napped.

When Ammi had been sick—*had* Ammi been sick? If she ever was—she did it quietly, so Noor wouldn't notice. Once, maybe, that Noor could remember, when her mother wasn't up and about to see Noor off to school and her father had said, 'Oh, your mother's not feeling well,' Noor had experienced a great stab of worry because what if Ammi *died*. And mothers weren't generally supposed to be ill. But by the time she came home, her mother was awake again, even bathed, ready to listen to Noor's account of her day. She was a bit like a cat—going and being sick in private, a very quiet, personal affair, which wouldn't intrude on the rest of them.

Obviously, the HOC as a patient was going to be even worse than the HOC was normally. Noor felt like she was going into war or something. Filled with righteousness, she set the kettle to boil and put water in a glass to carry in to her grandmother. She felt like she was exuding some sort of holy trail. She even imagined having conversations with people where she said, 'I just have to look after my grandmother. It is my duty.' Noor paused at the HOC's door to wipe some imaginary sweat off her forehead. Duty was *hard*.

'Gudiya?' The HOC's voice floated out to Noor. 'Are you there?'

'Yes, Daadi,' said Noor, carrying the water tray in. The HOC was sitting up in bed, her normally neat hair dishevelled, the fan spinning at the lowest speed, so each time it rotated, it groaned. The room *smelled* sick too, in a way that was hard to explain. Sort of closed and unaired and like the air was thick with viruses.

'Dad said you weren't feeling well.'

'But now he's gone off to work instead of taking care
of me. Works too hard, that man.' The HOC sighed and
gestured to Noor to put the tray down by her bed. 'I will die
soon anyway, and then you'll all be rid of this old woman.'
She sort of muttered that last bit to herself, like she wasn't
expecting a response, and Noor ignored her, reaching out
instead, to place her palm on the HOC's forehead like Ammi
used to do for her. She wasn't sure what the HOC's forehead
normally felt like, but now her skull throbbed into Noor's
palm, hot and fragile, like an egg.

'Turn on the radio, would you?' said the HOC. 'I feel like
listening to some music today. Something soft and nice from
my time. Those were good times, the music had a *tone* to
it—and fetch me my pills from that top drawer.'

Noor went to the dresser and opened it, pulling out a
blue strip of paracetamol. She then turned to the radio, so
ancient looking, she couldn't figure out how to operate it.

'Just turn it on,' said the HOC impatiently and coughed
a dry cough. Noor reached behind for the plug and put it in.
The radio must have been pre-tuned to an old Bollywood
station because, sure enough, old songs filtered through.
She personally didn't find any of old Hindi music appealing,
but her grandmother leaned back against her pillows again,
her eyes closed and—was she actually *smiling*? Well, well! So
maybe the lovelorn message the male singer was crooning
was triggering the HOC's long-dead romance button. Noor
smiled a little at the thought and then went to hand her
the pills.

The HOC opened her eyes and held on to Noor's wrist
with a surprisingly strong grip. 'Sit, no, Gudiya,' she said in

Hindi. 'We never got a chance to do this, you and I. By the time I learned you were born, we were already not talking to your father. But you are my first grandchild. How I longed to come and take you in my arms!'

'Take your pill, Daadi,' said Noor, almost gently. It wouldn't do for the HOC to get worked up.

The HOC took the pills and swallowed and just kept on talking. 'I wanted to call you Divya but your mother objected. Of course, every woman has a right to pick the name for her own child, but Noor! What sort of name is Noor?'

Noor began to get up, rolling her eyes. Once an HOC, always an HOC.

'Don't go, beta,' said the HOC, almost pleading. 'I feel the need to talk this morning. You know, your father sent me photographs after your first birthday. So many photographs! A whole big envelope of them! They came in a brown package, and your Chacha was the one to bring them to me and put them in my lap. "See Mummyji," he said. "See, your grandchild is here." We had to do it in private so that your grandfather wouldn't see them.'

Noor fiddled with her hair but she was listening intently, avidly. This was a part of the story no one had ever told her.

'He was a good man, your grandfather, but he was so set in his ways,' said the HOC, sensing her storytelling advantage. 'And I don't blame him. Your firstborn son is your firstborn son! Imagine if everyone wanted to have their own way? How would the world function? You are too young to understand this now but one day you will.'

She took a big sip of water and regarded Noor with a smug expression on her face, like, '*See*, I totally got you to sit still and listen to my stories.'

'When I was your age,' the HOC went on, 'they all called me headstrong—*zidd ke bachche*. I never wanted to do anything my elders and betters wanted me to do. If they said do this, I would do THAT. If my mother wanted me to learn singing, I wanted to go play cricket with my brothers.'

It was funny, she was speaking in Hindi, a language Noor knew but wasn't super fluent in, and yet, the words went through her brain without Noor even having to translate them in her head to English—that one step putting a gap between her and all native Hindi speakers.

'I used to be quite the bowler! You never thought that about your grandmother, did you? I remember when my mother wanted me to embroider a—what do you call them? Those fancy things that people put on top of their radios?— one of those as a showpiece for my aunt, her sister. I never liked my aunt then, may she rest in peace, but that woman was always going on and on and ON about the kind of girl I was. "*Ziddi* to the core," she told my poor mother. "This girl will NEVER learn or find a good husband." I found a better husband than her daughter did, and I wanted to say, "See? So much for my being wilful."'

She coughed a bit. 'Could I have a cup of tea, Gudiya? If it's not too much trouble for an old woman . . .' She let her voice trail off and looked pathetic, but managed to shout an order about how much sugar she should put and how strong she wanted her tea when Noor left the room.

When Noor returned with the tea, her grandmother had fallen asleep, so she left the tea by her bedside and went upstairs to surf the internet for a bit. Before long, she had dozed off as well and only woke up with a start an hour later.

She went downstairs again and poked her head into her grandmother's room. The HOC was awake and grumpy at having been neglected. 'Stone cold, this tea,' she said, making a sour-lemon face. 'Stone cold. And I've been calling for you and you didn't hear me.'

'I was napping,' said Noor, also feeling sulky and defensive.

'Well, I'd like another cup,' said the HOC. 'And turn off that radio, it's making my head hurt.'

Noor resisted the urge to give her the Nazi salute and stomped off to the kitchen to make some tea. By the time the kettle was boiling, she felt a little less irritable. The HOC was old after all and horribleness was probably in her nature. Besides, people were just generally more grumpy when they were sick. Noor decided to indulge her grandmother more, ask her for more stories, maybe that way she'd feel better.

'Did you make the embroidery thing for your aunt?' asked Noor when she returned. The HOC showed an inclination to sulk but, evidently, her desire to tell her story overcame that.

'Oh yes. My mother also wanted to show off my skills to her sister. She was a good woman, a modest, decent woman, but also prideful. It was something that my father didn't like about her.' Here, the HOC stopped to shake her head at her mother's follies. 'But who can blame her?

I was well known for my embroidery. All the girls I went to school with came over later, when they were going to get married and said, 'Will you embroider my dupatta? Will you put that latest-style embroidery on my sari pallu?' And then, they'd come back when they had babies: 'Will you make this hat for my baby? Will you make a hanky I can pin to his shirt?' As if I had no other work. Still. I did what I could do.' She glanced at Noor. 'I've done some embroidery on your cousin's jeans-pants before.'

'Oh wow,' said Noor. Embroidered jeans were always so expensive online. 'Maybe you could do one for me?'

'Maybe,' said the HOC. 'But anyway, my Amrita Mausi had two fears—she was afraid of bees and terrified of drowning. She had almost drowned once when she was two years old—they had all gone on a family trip and my grandfather took her into the sea in his arms and the wave splashed her. She called that "drowning". Stupid woman.' She took a big sip of her tea and said, 'Ahh. This is nice tea, Gudiya.'

Noor recognised this as a peace offering and tried not to smile.

'Well, ever since then, she avoided water altogether,' said the HOC. 'She was lucky we lived away from the sea. My mama, my mother's younger brother, lived in Calcutta, and there's a lot of water over there. She never visited him. My mother called this all drama but never to her face. My mother was a proud woman, no, and her pride extended to her family as well. She thought having a good family background meant that you were scared of certain things, as a woman should be. She is the one who taught me how to be shy and afraid. Otherwise, I never knew. It is a good lesson to have, Gudiya. Men like women who seem modest, like they want to hide away from the world. How else will men feel special?'

Noor considered her relationship with Ishaan. *She* hadn't been particularly modest. She giggled. 'What's so funny?' asked the HOC, but luckily, seemed more interested in carrying on with her own story.

'Every husband should feel that for his wife, he is the only man in the world. That's my lesson to you. Even though, once you have a son, your son is everything, you should never let your husband know that. That is why I had to hide that envelope with your photos from your grandfather, even though my heart was crying—CRYING—for my son. I hope you never know such unhappiness. I don't know what sin I was atoning for, but it must have been something in my past life.' Her eyes filled with tears and Noor sort of felt bad for her. Poor old HOC. It *must* have been sort of hard to live without her son.

'Muslims don't believe in a past life, do they, Gudiya? I wondered that about your mother. How would she KNOW what to do if, say, God forbid, my son died before her?' Her grandmother dabbed at the corners of her eyes with her sari pallu. 'She wouldn't know how to put his soul to rest. Like should marry like. Imagine if a peacock married a sparrow! I was afraid for my poor son, what sin did *he* commit? What will his next life be like? Ah, I hope I am, at least, freed from this earthly burden soon.'

Noor didn't know much about what Islam felt about reincarnation, so she couldn't contradict her grandmother.

But still, it was a lonely feeling—if her father's side was right and they were all going to be reborn over and over again, and her mother, stubborn-willed and *Muslim*, were to stay put where she was. An eternity without Ammi.

'And they wear the veil also,' said the HOC, still continuing her meditations on religion. 'What if *they* took your father into that world? What if he became a terrorist or one of those people who wanted four wives or didn't believe in marriage at all? Just one *talaq talaq talaq* and they can kick their wives to the door, you know. Us Hindus, we have a long culture of respecting women. Some people say we don't, but then, we believe if a woman is in the home and she is a good wife, then there is no need for another. What is all this four wives business? It's unlawful is what it is.'

'By *they*, you mean my mother's family, Daadi?' asked Noor. Whether the HOC was sick or not, this was Noor's chance to defend the people she loved.

The HOC shot her a sharp look. 'I don't know about all that, Gudiya. I never met them. They never came to my house with sweets to celebrate their daughter's marriage to my son.'

Because you'd probably kick them out of the house, thought Noor, but made a 'mmm' sound to indicate she was listening.

'Your grandfather was sick, poor man, and then your father came into the house—this house your grandfather's father had built with his own two hands—and your father was like a ray of sunshine, my son after so long with an empty womb. And your grandfather started to feel better almost immediately.' The HOC actually shone with her remembered joy at that memory and Noor rolled her eyes.

My grandfather still sounds kind of douchey, she said to herself as the HOC continued. 'He sat up in bed and asked for tea to be brought, and his spectacles, and your father bent down and touched his feet and I thought, "Good, the boy has not lost his way even though he lives in Bombay." What did I know of the sorrows life would bring me? Ah well, he lived a good life. And we never know what fate has in store for us. Your father brought you to see me, and I had the photographs.'

Noor made a little start at this information.

'Oh, didn't you know?' asked the HOC innocently. 'Yes, you were about two years old and we had come to Delhi for a wedding. Your father dressed you up and brought you out of the house. Your mother was working, of course. A working woman cannot look after both her job and her family. You remember that, Gudiya.'

Noor rolled her eyes again. If she rolled them much more, they'd probably fall out of her sockets and lie on the ground. 'I have to go do my homework now, Daadi,' she said, just to escape.

The HOC waved her away, apparently happy to just sit back and think about the past by herself. Noor got to the door and remembered she hadn't heard the end of one story. 'What embroidery did you make for your mausi finally?'

The HOC smiled to herself at that long-ago memory. 'I made her the showpiece, the most beautiful showpiece that anyone had ever seen. I worked for a full week on it and begged my parents to buy me the new, fancy thread that cost more money than the old ones. But in the end, everyone agreed it was beautiful.'

'Oka-ay?'

'It was—let me see, yes, I remember—it was a beautiful picture of a waterfall and right next to it, a big, big, *big* beehive. I did that in golden and brown and yellow.'

'Did she ever use it?'

'Well now, yes she did, bitiya.' The HOC's eyes glinted. 'She had to. I spent so much time on it. She kept it for many years on her front table.'

Noor turned, a bit bewildered but still fascinated at this image of her grandmother as a rebellious teen pressing upon her hated aunt a picture of the things she was most scared of and would have to live with forever. It was sort of radical.

Actually, it was sort of *cool*.

She turned to go up the stairs again and then remembered, 'Daadi, no one in my mother's family has four wives or wears a veil. Not everyone is the way you think they are.'

Instantly, the HOC's mouth shrivelled and she began to rustle through her prayer book with great urgency. Noor knew she wouldn't get a reply and left, but she thought later, as she lay in bed, that it was so sad that the HOC had to turn into the HOC. At sixteen, her grandmother sounded like someone Noor would have been friends with. She sounded *nice*. And *reasonable*. All things the HOC wasn't now.

Old people were *weird*.

*

Ishaan to Noor, text message 1

Hello! Didn't see you at school today?

Noor to Ishaan, text message 2

Ugh, I had to nurse my grandmother. Did I miss anything?

Ishaan to Noor, text message 3

Fascinating stuff, as usual. Two guys who looked like gorillas had a face-off in the parking lot.

Noor to Ishaan, text message 4

OMG! I miss all the fun stuff! LOL! Why were they fighting?

Ishaan to Noor, text message 5

Do you actually lol when you 'LOL'?

Noor to Ishaan, text message 6

What are you, the LOL police? And you didn't answer my q . . .

Ishaan to Noor, text message 7

About why they were fighting? From what I could gather, Gorilla with the unibrow made a pass at Gorilla with the overbite's girlfriend. And yes, as your boyfriend, I am also your LOL police. Don't LOL if you don't actually LOL.

Ishaan to Noor, text message 8

So, you haven't written back to my last message. I'm guessing it's because you hate the LOL police. Fine, fine, I'll settle for being the LOL supervisor.

Noor to Ishaan, text message 9

Hmmmm.

Ishaan to Noor, text message 10

I thought I'd work the 'boyfriend' thing in subtly. Did it work?

Noor to Ishaan, text message 11

How do you know I even WANT to be your girlfriend?

Ishaan to Noor, text message 12

Do you want to be my girlfriend?

Noor to Ishaan, text message 13

Ishaan to Noor, text message 14

The phone rang right before dinner was set and Noor's father picked it up. He sounded terse and Noor assumed it was a work call. If there was one thing her father hated, it was phone calls at meal times. It bothered him more than you would think was normal. It, like, *really* bothered him, and he often grumbled that people should look at the clock more when they reached out for the phone. 'It's not a phone, it's a *leash*,' he used to say. 'Whoever invented the cell phone can go on about how amazing it is that you can connect with anyone at any time but that's just it—you can connect to *anyone* at *any time*.' Noor used to laugh at this but now she sort of got what he meant. If she had known that their last family dinner was going to be their last—maybe she would have spent more time treasuring it. Not the *last*-last, but the last one where everything was still normal. What had they been eating? What had her mother said and what had her father replied? Had there been a phone call that evening to snatch away even those precious few minutes of them being a normal family before everything vanished?

'Noor.' Her father nodded towards the phone. 'For you.'

'Oh?' she looked up from where she was playing a game on her phone. 'Who is it?'

Her father just shook his head and went back to the dining table, where he had been reading, and picked up his book, lying face down on the surface.

'Hello?'

At the other end of the receiver, static. And then, a familiar voice said, 'Noorie?'

'Nana!'

It was her grandfather. Beloved Nana. Her mother's father, who had always treated her as an adult, even when she was very small. Her first memory of him was how, one summer, he had taken her to see the lights on Marine Drive. He had taken her to a particular spot and told her to look down the whole bay.

'What does it look like, Noorie?'

'It looks like a necklace!'

'It does, doesn't it? A necklace of lights around the throat of Bombay.'

Often, he had said things like that, things she hadn't completely understood at the time, but words which she grew to treasure over the years. Nana was also Nana to her two cousins, her mother's sister's daughters, who, at twenty-one and nineteen, didn't seem to need him that much anymore. He was Dada to her uncle's son, who was thirteen and spent most of his time outdoors, no matter what the weather. But Noor had, somehow, always known she was her grandfather's favourite. Not that he had ever said so, of course; Nana was a very diplomatic man. But they shared a secret sense, a way of being around each other that assured the other person that this was exactly where they wanted to be, with whom they wanted to be.

'Noorie, I wanted to call you earlier, but . . .' Nana's voice trailed off, and Noor suddenly felt angry at her mother for putting her grandfather through all this. Imagine Nana faltering for a word! He never stumbled, never said 'um' or 'err', and this hurt in his voice was all Ammi's fault.

''Sokay, Nana,' said Noor, glancing towards the dining table. Her father and the HOC had ostensibly started eating, but she knew they were listening hard.

'I wanted to, you know, show my *support* to you in this difficult time.'

'I know.'

'Roxy was always so wilful.'

This, oddly, reminded Noor of the HOC's story. *Zidd ke bachche*. The HOC and Ammi having the same personality? How strange everything was today.

'I'm fine, Nana.'

'Are you really? Your Nani and I were talking and we think you should come to Bombay when your holidays start. I'll send you a ticket. You need to be with family, Noorie.'

'I *am* with family, though, Nana.'

'You know what I mean.' He coughed a bit. He used to be a smoker, a two-pack-a-day habit he had kicked five years ago, but every now and then, he smoked a pipe, and that stayed in his cough.

Through the glass pane of the dining room door, Noor could see her father. The lines around his mouth made his face droop, his eyes immensely sad. She felt a bit like weeping. Poor Dad. He had never been enough in the world of Ammi-and-Noor, their little club excluding him. Even though he was always there in her memories and in real life, Dad was somehow a faded-out figure, a pencil sketch in front of her mother's permanent marker. And even now, after Ammi was gone, the big black hole that she left—that lingered on her side of the table, that came up when Noor thought about Bombay—that big black hole was more *present* for Noor than her dad was. She wanted, absurdly, to defend him, to tell her Nana that her father was enough family for her, but the truth was he *wasn't*. He hadn't even spoken to Noor about anything. They just stepped around the giant elephant in the room, occasionally feeding it peanuts.

'Noorie?'

'Sorry, Nana, I zoned out for a sec there.'

'About Bombay, you will come, yes? I told your mother I would ask you.'

Ammi. He spoke to Ammi. *Of course* he had spoken to Ammi. It was ridiculous that he wouldn't, and yet, and yet, this all felt like such a betrayal. This was *her* Nana, a person who loved her more than most people, and he had practically gone over to enemy camp.

'You spoke to my mother?'

A long sigh. Nana knew what was up. 'She called me the other day. She was worried about you. You haven't been replying to her emails.' This last said somewhat accusatorily.

'I didn't *want* to reply to her emails.'

'Noorie . . .'

'No, Nana, you don't understand. She just walked out on us, like nothing was the matter. She just *walked out*. She just *left*.' Tears were now prickling the top of her nose, like the fizz in a cold drink.

'My darling, I know it's hard.'

'You *don't* know!'

'So tell me then.'

Noor felt immensely tired. She *couldn't* be thinking about all this. She had other things to think about (a boyfriend, for instance). She was so exhausted with her mother spinning around in her brain all day, like her brain was a washing machine set to one speed and you couldn't ever pull out the load.

'I don't want to talk about it.'

'If you met Sunny . . .' A pause. 'You know, I know it's the hardest on you but this kind of love is one you meet only once in your lifetime. Your parents haven't been happy together for a long time, baby, and Sunny appeared at a point when things were not so good for your mother.'

'How do *you* know they weren't happy? They *seemed* happy to me.'

'Because she told me, no. Your mother is also my daughter. I know her moods. I've known her since she was born and I know how hard a decision this was for her to make. But if she had stayed, even if she had stayed for your sake—which she wanted to do—she wouldn't be your Ammi anymore. She'd be someone else.'

A memory. Just two months before Ammi left. They were all sitting around the living room, Noor watching TV, her parents reading. Noor had turned her head to ask her mother something and caught her in a moment where her face was open, unguarded, full of despair. Noor hadn't understood it then and she didn't fully understand it now, but some inner saving voice had made her talk very loudly and cheerfully about the show and her mother had rearranged her features and smiled and laughed along. However, that moment, that expression, it could never be erased.

Still, it was so selfish of her to leave.

Noor cleared her throat. 'I *said* I didn't want to talk about it!'

'Fair enough,' said her grandfather, 'but I hope you're talking to someone.'

'I have a group at school.'

'Okay. I'll back off then. Now, about Bombay.'

'Yes, I guess I'll come.'

'Splendid!' Nana's voice turned into a smile and Noor could imagine him, sitting by the phone table—her grandparents refused to get a cordless phone and only just barely remembered to charge their cell phones—and drumming on the carved wood, the way he did when he was really pleased. 'Will you message me your holiday dates?'

'I will, Nana.'

'Goodbye then, Noorie. God bless you.'

She put down the phone and turned to find herself face to face with Dad, who had given up the pretence of not listening. 'Hi Dad?' she said, getting up to step around him.

'Go where?' he asked.

'Nana–Nani want me to go to Bombay for my summer holiday.'

'Absolutely not.'

Noor was stunned into silence. What? Her dad couldn't stop her from seeing her grandparents, could he?

'He can't just *demand* you go there like you're some

orphan! I am your parent too, Noor, and as your *only* parent, I don't like the idea of you traipsing around Bombay alone.'

'Um, hello? I wouldn't be alone. I'd be with Nana–Nani.'

'And we all know what a good influence they are!' Her father was breathing really heavily now, his nostrils flaring. 'No, you can't go. I want you to come to Jaipur and meet my family. You've already spent too many years with those people.'

Aghast and furious, Noor faced him, her hands balled into fists. 'That's not fair! I don't want to go to Jaipur!'

'Well, that's just too damn bad! You don't have a choice! You have more than one family and I insist you keep your obligations.'

Noor didn't know whether she was more taken aback by the fact that he had said 'damn' (parents weren't supposed to swear!) or that he was actually doing this, actually forbidding her from seeing her grandparents.

'Now go inside and eat your dinner,' he said, which made her even madder. Eat her dinner like absolutely nothing had happened? No way!

'I'm not *hungry* and you *can't* do this.' She thought of threatening him by saying she'd tell her mother but that was ridiculous because her mother wasn't here. Her father was. And he was making her go to Jaipur and give up everything and be with his horrible, horrible family, all of whom were probably just as bad, if not worse than the HOC. She gave a strangled sob and dashed up the stairs to her room, banging the door so hard that it bounced off the frame and she had to get up and close it again.

She hated them. She hated them *all*.

7

'Is there anything as fake as paneer?' mused Armana, holding up a roll she had been handed. 'I mean, this is pretend chicken. It's so the vegetarians can feel better about themselves not eating chicken, but they're so desperate to try some real protein, they're disguising their gross cubes of dairy.'

'Shhhh!' whispered Sonum, nudging her. 'Pooja might hear!'

Pooja, a girl in their class, was distributing kathi rolls and laddus to celebrate her birthday, something none of them had done since they were about ten. Twelve at the *latest*. Pooja wore the harried, flushed expression of a hostess at a dinner party who just wants to get everyone *fed* and *happy* so she can go somewhere and eat in peace. The boys were accepting her food (Hey! Free!) with great glee but the girls—not just the Group—were looking at it slightly askance. Even Pooja's friends, who were helping her, looked slightly apologetic as they handed out the wrapped rolls ('They're *all* paneer,' one of them said regretfully, as one of the boys asked for chicken.) and laddus on paper plates.

Noor looked at her roll. Blech. The onions and green chutney, normally such an appealing combination, looked cold and accusing. The smell even turned her stomach a little bit. 'I can't eat this,' she said, pushing it aside. 'Does anyone want it?'

'*I can't eat this*,' said Armana, sing-songing an imitation of Noor's voice. '*I'm just a sad little girl and I can't eat anything because I'm so sad.*'

Noor blinked at her. Sonum started to laugh but in a weird, mean way. Natasha avoided eye contact and Sanvi wasn't there or maybe Sanvi would have stopped them.

'What?' asked Noor.

'*Stupid says what?*' Renewed cackling from Sonum.

'You guys,' said Natasha, shaking her head but *not actually saying anything to stop it.*

'Can you just tell me what's going on?'

'No, darling Noor, *you* tell us what's going on,' said Armana, waving her unwrapped roll for emphasis. 'You've been acting really weird lately. And my *sources* tell me there's some *guy*.' Her lip curled with scorn and amusement. As if Noor could get a guy on her own who was superior in any way, said her expression. As if Noor was smart enough to make her own decisions.

'Your *sources* being *that* one, I guess,' said Noor, shooting Sonum a dirty look. Oh, why did they all have to pretend to still like Sonum? She was horrible! Noor wanted to reach out and smack that smug expression off her face. It was all Sonum's fault. Sonum, with her greasy pink lips and her Brazilian blow-out hair barely disguising her sticking-out ears.

Sonum shook her hair back, surely reading the contempt on Noor's face, and said, 'Wrong!'

'It wasn't Sonum,' said Armana. 'Never mind who my sources are. Why didn't you tell us you had a *boyfriend*?' She managed to make 'boyfriend' sound lame and childish, like a Barbie doll.

'It's so not a big deal,' said Noor. She glanced at Natasha for help but Natasha only looked hurt. 'You didn't tell me you were seeing someone,' she said.

'It just sort of happened. Besides, I'm not acting weird.'

'Oh yeah? Well, you're, like, flaking on us all the time. If there's something else going on that's more important to you than your friends, let us know so we won't keep bothering you,' said Armana, dropping her roll so it fell and bounced on the ground.

'Yeah, Noor,' Sonum was hands-on-hips now, *loving* this. 'Meher was just saying the other day that she'd love to come to one of our movie nights.'

'I like Meher,' said Armana, 'I'm sure she has time for her friends and doesn't spend all *her* time with boys.'

It struck Noor how incredibly unfair this was, as any time Reansh had free, Armana would spend with him, even cancelling on premade plans with them last minute so she could go to his house and make out. She even sent cheery group messages, 'Sorry ladies! But a girl's gotta do . . .' And none of them had resented it—well, not *much*—because it was understood that when you had a boyfriend, he sort of took priority over everything else. It was a grown-up thing, having a boyfriend, and you had to be able to put aside childish things like hanging out with your friends.

Armana used to say heavily, 'One day, you'll understand,' while patting Noor on the head and Noor suddenly realized that the rules that applied to Armana didn't necessarily apply to her as well.

Reprieve came in the shape of Sanvi, walking towards them and waving.

'Sorry guys! I had to finish this thing for class,' she sat down and glanced at the fallen roll. 'Did I miss all the goodies?'

'You can have mine,' said Noor, thrusting her roll into Sanvi's hand. 'I've lost my appetite.'

'Because she only has appetite for *one* thing,' said Sonum, and Armana laughed.

'Would you just *shut up*?' said Noor, turning to Sonum, her eyes narrowed with hate. She was clenching her jaw so hard, her teeth squeaked against each other.

'Why should she shut up?' asked Armana, quick as a wink. They had planned this, Noor thought slowly. They had planned everything, down to how they would give her a hard time.

'Yeah,' said Sonum, looking the calmest and most confident Noor had ever seen her because Armana was actively on her side. '*You* don't like the discussion, *you* go somewhere else.'

'Maybe I will,' said Noor, glancing at Sanvi and Natasha to see if any help at all was coming from that quarter. Sanvi just looked surprised to be in the middle of this and Natasha was drawing a pattern in the dust with the tip of her shoe.

'Fine,' said Noor, her eyes blurry with tears. 'Fine, I'm leaving.'

'Okay bye-eee,' caroled Sonum, and she and Armana cracked up laughing as Noor walked away, feeling the loneliest she ever had in her life.

The third-floor girls' toilet had a number of advantages over its lower-floor counterparts. For one, this was the board-exam floor, only class X and XII were allowed, so the halls were hushed, with no noises to mask the sound of approaching footsteps. For another, it was a large bathroom, and fairly new. Instead of the swing-gate cubicles of the lower floors, the third-floor bathroom had actual doors and smelled of deodorizer instead of sweat. There was a handicapped stall in the back—the school's nod to the differently abled, even though there weren't any students who needed it—and it was there that Noor sought refuge, sitting on the pot and weeping into her hands.

She cried until she couldn't cry anymore and then just waited there to compose herself. It would have helped to talk to someone, but whom? Ishaan was still too new in her life to unload all of this on. Besides, there was the delicate matter that the fight was sort of about him, and how would she convey all of this to him without hurting his feelings or avoiding being asked really obvious questions like 'Why didn't you just tell them about me?' Ironically, she couldn't express her emotions about it to anyone outside the Group. The feeling of being lesser-than, the feeling of being picked on, the feeling that if she gave them the information they wanted, she'd be even more vulnerable than before. 'But they're your *friends*,' Ishaan would argue, and she didn't know quite how to articulate that yes, they were her friends, but also they were not. They could close in on you like a school of piranhas. At times, they were the best friends a girl could ever have and at other times, you had to try really hard to navigate their sharp, stabby voices and thin-as-ice social protocol so you wouldn't fall through and hurt yourself.

She could hear feet approaching in the corridor outside and she pulled into herself and tried not to sniffle, as the door opened and someone checked all the cubicles. When the footsteps neared her cubicle, she held her breath and waited. The hand tried the door and then a familiar voice said, 'Noor? Are you in here?'

It was Sanvi. Funny how it was Sanvi who came to find her and not Natasha. It should have been Natasha. God knows she had cried in front of Natasha before and vice versa. Natasha's grandmother had died. Noor had been at Natasha's house and she had just laid her head on Noor's lap and wept. And Noor had said nothing, just stroked her hair and waited for her to finish crying. You would think something like that would draw people closer together. You would think that bond would be stronger than the siren call of Armana's perfect, glamorous life, full of parties and beautiful clothes and interesting things.

She opened the door and Sanvi came in. 'Oh, Noor,' she said sadly, taking in Noor's puffy, teary eyes and downturned mouth. She wasn't a very touchy-feely person, so when she put her arms around Noor for an awkward hug, Noor felt absurdly touched and began to cry again.

'I didn't *mean* to keep it from you guys,' she managed between sniffles. Sanvi was sitting on the clean floor of the bathroom (another point in favour of the third-floor loo) and handing her toilet paper.

'I know you didn't,' Sanvi murmured soothingly. 'Sometimes, these things happen, man. You don't want to just go around blabbing to people all the time. Armana and them need to grow up.'

This was new. She had never considered herself as more adult than Armana or Natasha, with their airs of adulthood. But yes, *maybe* it *was* more mature to keep a thing to yourself instead of blabbing to the whole world that you wanted a boyfriend. Take *that*, Natasha.

'Do you want to tell me about him?' asked Sanvi.

'It's that guy, Ishaan. I told you about him already. The new guy?'

'Oh yeah, at Bagga's house, right? He seemed cool.'

'Well, I guess we sort of made it official?'

'Wow!' Sanvi smiled at Noor. 'Look at you taking matters into your own hands.'

Noor sighed. 'I know we discuss these things but, you know, it just *happened*.'

'Hey,' Sanvi took Noor's hands and looked her right in the eye. 'You can't take all this Group stuff seriously, man. I mean, it's nice to *have*, but then you've also gotta have your own shit going on, you know?'

Noor nodded but she didn't really get it, and Sanvi understood because she said, 'This stuff with Armana and Sonum and even Natasha—though I know you, like, *love* her—it's just *stuff*. What's important is your life and doing your own thing.'

'You must really love Aryan,' Noor said, looking at Sanvi's shining eyes. Sanvi laughed. 'Oh, he's okay, but really, Noor, who I love is myself. I know that sounds, like, *hugely* arrogant but I like who I am, you know. Would I change some things about my life? Sure. But I like who I am, I like Aryan—hell, maybe I even love Aryan—and that makes it easy for me to cut through the bullshit.'

'You're so brave, Sanvi,' said Noor. She wished she could be more like her friend, sitting there with the bright tube light of the bathroom diffused in her hair so the light streaked down towards her face, her eyes smiling, her mouth pensive. Sanvi was like that—she took no prisoners and she didn't put up with stuff. And finally, *finally*, Noor got how Sanvi was so much cooler than everyone else.

'Noor?' said Sanvi

'Yeah?'

'Is there anything else going on with you?'

All defences up. 'What do you mean?'

'You haven't been yourself at all lately and I know it's not just the boyfriend stuff. Is something bothering you?'

For a minute, Noor considered telling her, just letting it all off her chest, but she didn't want to deal, didn't want to think about it. She wanted to let it go and telling someone else meant one more person asking if she was okay, if she had spoken to her mother, if she was still fighting with her father, and on and on and on the questions would go. And it was easier holding up the load herself.

'I'm *fine*,' she said, sharper than she had intended but Sanvi didn't look hurt or surprised. Instead, she put her hand on Noor's knee and said, 'I'm here any time you want to talk. I mean it too—it's not just one of those things.'

'Hmm,' said Noor, and then, to change the subject and also because she wanted to know how much stuff to deal with, she asked, 'Do Armana and Sonum and Natasha hate me now?'

'Eh,' Sanvi shrugged. 'They'll get over it. You and I can hang in the meanwhile. I was getting tired of seeing Natasha run around behind Armana anyway. This is a great loo, Noor'—looking around—'I begin to see why you chose it for your weep spot.'

Noor giggled and the conversation turned to Sanvi's family—how her brother and sister-in-law wanted to move to a new home, which Sanvi thought was a great idea but which her parents saw as a massive betrayal. There were tears and people weeping and the toddler nephew picked up and hugged by all quarters . . . Noor was feeling quite herself by the time the bell rang again.

'Tchah, Maths!' said Sanvi, getting up reluctantly. 'Why can't all days have library or free periods? Hey, you want to hang out after school today?'

'I can't,' Noor said. She was going to Ankur's birthday party, although she half wondered if she could miss it. But then, she remembered his eager little face and the fact that she had bought him a present, a DIY model kit of a dinosaur which she thought he'd appreciate.

'Ishaan stuff?' asked Sanvi, knowingly, and Noor nodded. 'Ishaan stuff.'

See, that's the one good thing about having a group of friends, she told the Ishaan in her head. There was always one friend who could be counted on to be amazing. She linked arms with Sanvi and they walked back to their classes.

*

'So are you ready for this?' asked Ishaan, as they pulled up to Ankur's house. It had taken them some time to find, winding through back lanes and alleys until they realized Ankur's hand-drawn map, printed on the back of his invitation, was totally off the scale and they just asked someone how to get there. Noor had texted her father for permission to attend that morning—she still wasn't speaking to him, so all her communication had been via SMS.

'Friend's birthday party after school. Mite b late.'
'Ok. Tell daadi.'

It was funny how she didn't use SMSese with anyone else except her parents, and that, only because her parents seemed to *expect* it of her. They even sent her SMSese back, a way to engage with her generation—or so they said to their friends at boring dinner parties, where everyone smelled of whiskey and laughed too much at things that weren't funny.

'I'm not exactly sure *what* I should be ready for,' said Noor, squeezing his hand. The worst of the tears were over, and after school, Sanvi had lent her some eye pencil and a quick fix of eye drops to make her eyes less puffy. She had brushed her hair till it protested with static and sprayed some floral, pink-bottled thing all over herself and changed into the clothes she had carried in her school bag—a pink floral top with tie-up straps and blue jeans—nothing too sexy for someone's twelfth birthday, but which gave her the illusion of a bust. She felt like someone who had never cried in a bathroom before, but her nerves were still slightly on edge, her stomach all jangly.

'Meeting people after school is always a little weird,' said Ishaan. He was so *nice*. He hadn't kept up a constant stream of chatter in the car either, sensing perhaps that today was not a good day. And Noor had appreciated the quiet time to collect her thoughts.

'I know, I wonder what Diya's like at a party,' she said, giggling a little out of nervousness.

'Diya's cool, though,' said Ishaan, swinging their hands between them, 'I mean, she makes me laugh. She's just so . . . so . . .'

'Argumentative? Rude?'

'Hah, no, I was going to say "strident", it's quite funny. She's sweet.'

Noor rolled her eyes privately. Sometimes Ishaan could be *too* nice.

Ankur's house was set between two larger 'builder' apartments, which were all glass balconies and high, imposing walls and smart watchmen waiting outside to let people in or out. In contrast, his house, which hugged the walls of the apartments on either side, was small and shabby, a two-floor family place, with a garden that, Noor noticed, had some limp-looking balloons hanging on a washing line across the grass. There was also a plastic table with some chips and Coke and Fanta in big plastic bottles, and some red plastic chairs arranged in lines, like they were waiting for a speech or something. Of everyone else there was no sign, but just then, Ankur came out and beamed at them.

'You came!' he said, delighted. His porcupine hair was sitting down for a change, and he was in a red check shirt that matched the garden chairs, and brown, long corduroy pants.

'Of course we came,' said Ishaan, dropping Noor's hand and reaching out for a high five, which Ankur returned with great gusto.

'And you came too!' he said, turning to Noor. 'I thought you wouldn't.'

'Why wouldn't I?' asked Noor, and Ankur did a full body shrug. 'Dunno.'

A woman came to the door, wearing a mustard-yellow salwar kameez. She looked tired and her hair was a bit messy, threaded through with strands of silver. 'Are your friends here?' she asked Ankur, before smiling at Noor and Ishaan. 'You must be his friends from the new group at school. Ankur can't stop talking about you all. Come in, have something cold.'

They went inside and sat in a crowded drawing room, full to the brim with sofa sets and curio cabinets and dark wood coffee tables. There was a dining table and six chairs squeezed into a corner, and it was there that they were ushered, where Diya and Saraswati already sat.

'Did you guys come straight from school?' asked Diya. 'I could have taken a ride with you.' She seemed to take them in, measuring them up, and surmised they were together. And she didn't seem to like what she saw very much because she conveyed all this with a slightly disapproving sniff.

'Is this all of us?' asked Noor, taking a seat at the table furthest from Diya.

'Yes, just us,' said Saraswati, who was wearing a pink, frilly frock and swinging her legs and looking much younger than she was. Her hair had been freshly braided for the occasion, and instead of the usual white or yellow ribbons, these were hot pink.

'My other friends don't want to come over anymore,' said Ankur, matter-of-factly. 'Their mummies won't let them come.'

Noor was startled by this information but Ankur looked so composed about it that she let it go and pulled out her present from her bag. 'I got you something,' she said.

'So did we *all*,' said Diya, shooting Noor a dirty look, as if by announcing a present first, she was taking credit for something that didn't belong to her.

'Presents later,' said Ankur's mother, who had just walked in again from the kitchen. 'How about some party games first?'

'I asked for Scrabble this year for my birthday!' said Ankur, looking at Ishaan adoringly. 'I said it was what the big boys played.'

'Thank you for getting him interested in words,' said Ankur's mother, smiling and putting her palm on top of Ankur's head. Something about her smile was sad though, thought Noor, as Ankur pulled out a set of Scrabble tiles, still shrink-wrapped, and began to rip into it. The house felt sorrowful, as if Ankur's mother was trying her hardest to open the windows and let the sun come in but it didn't stand a chance against the metal grill firmly fixed to each window.

They played for a while. Ankur's mother brought out chips and passed them around in plastic bowls. 'Why don't any of your friends like to come over anymore?' asked Saraswati suddenly. It was a question very unlike Saraswati. Noor knew they had all come together because all of their parents had split up, but with Saraswati—well, you couldn't imagine her making a fuss when her parents fought or being sulky when she was being driven away in a car in the opposite direction from the house she grew up in. Someone must care for her, the ribbons in her hair were evidence of that, but she seemed like an entity in and of herself, out of reach from any conflict.

'They saw my daddy fighting with my mummy,' said Ankur, casually, tapping a 'Q' against his two front teeth. 'He'd been—*you know*.' He curled his hand into a fist, extended the thumb and pretended to pour the thumb into his mouth. 'He called it his medicine. Daddy said it wasn't shameful to have if you had a reason, like he did. He was sad. Oh cool, I got a 'U'! Ha-*HAH!* Diya-di, looks like I might beat you after all!'

Noor glanced around at everyone but no one said anything. Diya tried weakly, 'In your dreams, kiddo!' but you could tell her heart wasn't really in it.

'My father just *left*,' said Saraswati sweetly. 'But at least he wasn't *fighting* with my mother.'

Ankur stuck his tongue out at her. 'Goody-goody for you!'

'Ankur, manners!' said his mother, who came in just then with a plate piled high with food. Diya, of course, leapt up to help her serve and Noor decided she might as well too, just so Ishaan wouldn't think she had terrible manners. She wasn't sure how much of the conversation Ankur's mother had heard but she seemed quite serene, if slightly hassled about catering to her guests' needs.

'Do you have any sisters or brothers?' asked Ankur's mother, after everyone had been seated with a purple-bordered plastic plate in front of them. And she took their plates one by one and served pulao, bordered with channa, added methi potatoes bursting out of their skin, and some chicken curry for anyone who wasn't vegetarian—which was everyone but Saraswati.

'I have a brother,' said Diya, and God, she liked to *participate* at parties as well. Was there no end to it? 'He's younger than me. He's at boarding school.' She looked a bit worried and said, 'He *wanted* to go. It's a tradition for the men in my family.'

'I have three younger sisters—Ahalya, Durga and Parvati,' said Saraswati, spearing a potato with her fork.

'Three! And you are the oldest?' asked Ankur's mother. Saraswati nodded. 'Do you help take care of them?'

'Yes,' said Saraswati. 'Sometimes, my mother, she can't look after all of us. So I do it.'

'That must be hard,' said Noor, putting her hand on Saraswati's, who blinked at her and said, 'No, not really. I'm used to it now. I can even do their hair like mine.' She shook out her braids and Noor said, 'Very pretty' because she was expected to say something. She thought how easy it was to

assume something about someone by the way they were
dressed, so fast had she just thought that Saraswati was a
younger sibling, if that, that a doting mother helped her on
with her clothes every morning, and brushed and braided
her hair and made sure she looked sweet and simple. But
when Noor looked closer, the hand she held had a small,
fresh-looking burn on it right above the knuckle and the
clothes weren't as fresh as she had first assumed, looking
both wrinkled and small, suddenly. The chest of the dress
was too tight—it strained—and the hem too short. It was
probably a younger sister's borrowed finery.

'I had two younger brothers,' said Ankur's mother, also
smiling at Saraswati but in this fixed way. 'I had to look after
them too. I wanted Ankur to have lots of brothers and sisters
too, but it is in God's hands, isn't it?'

Well, God's hands and kinda your own too, thought Noor,
and then got the giggles, which she hurriedly buried in her
water glass. She looked over at Ishaan, who winked at her.

'What about *you*, Noor?' said Diya, loudly, 'Do *you* have
any siblings?'

'Um, no, I don't. And there's no need to shout, Diya, I'm,
like, right here. I can hear you.'

'Well, we don't KNOW anything ABOUT you, Noor. You
may as well be a ROBOT. Do you have anything to SAY or
is all of this just stuff you LAUGH with your friends about?'

Ankur's mother had left the table to clear up, Ankur and
Saraswati were sharing a joke over something, and Ishaan
was in the other room making a phone call. It was just her
and Diya.

'CAT got your TONGUE?' asked Diya, smirking, 'MORE

stuff to cry at home about? I mean, are your PARENTS even DIVORCED? Poor little rich girl, it must be SO, SO HARD to deal with all the LOSERS around you, right? I know Saras made you come, she TOLD me. And I know you weren't going to come back, only, you wanted a BOYFRIEND. So why don't you stop pretending and just get REAL about it?'

'What. Is. Your. Problem?' Noor got out through clenched teeth. This was just turning into that day, she thought to herself and almost laughed. Could anything else go wrong?

'My problem is *you*, you entitled little bitch,' said Diya, coming really close and pushing Noor in the chest with one finger. 'You never share. You don't care about anything. You're just collecting information to laugh about us later with your friends.'

'That's not true!'

'Oh yeah? I've seen your friends and you. I know you laugh at me. What's to stop you from laughing at them as well?' She jerked her head towards Ankur and Saraswati who looked scared.

'We don't laugh at you,' said Noor, guiltily, but Diya was too far gone in her rage. 'Prove it. PROVE it then. Say something about your life, *anything*.'

'I . . . can't.'

'I knew it.' Diya turned around and faced Ankur. 'Don't tell Noor *anything* about your life. She's just going to make fun of you later.'

'Noor didi?' Ankur looked puzzled and hurt. 'Why?'

'Don't listen to her, Ankur! She's crazy!'

'Then why don't we know anything about your life? I bet

even your *boyfriend* doesn't know, do you, Ishaan?' Ishaan had stepped out and was looking at the scene with horror.

'Stop it, Diya,' he said at once.

'I'm going home,' said Noor.

'Typical! Run, run, princess, go home to your palace-with-no-problems-at-all.'

Noor suddenly got completely sick of it. Fuck this. Fuck them. Fuck her parents. 'You want to know about my palace, Diya? My palace is this apartment with my dad and his mother, who is absolutely horrible and can't stop bad mouthing my mother because she's Muslim. My grandmother hates Muslims, which means she probably hates me for being half-Muslim. My *mother* left—yeah, you got your mother? All of you have your mothers, but *my* mother decided she'd rather be with an old boyfriend than with her daughter, so how's that for rejection? Palace enough for you?'

She ran out of breath and just stood there, watching dismay wash across Ishaan's face and mutinous guilt across Diya's. Just then, a tinny recording of *Happy Birthday To You* started playing and Ankur's mother walked in, holding a cake, her face lit up by candles. Noor couldn't take it anymore, so she left, closing the door behind her and walking as fast as she could, till she saw an auto. She flagged it down and sat inside, trembling.

8

The happy, jazzy tune chimed again, going on and on for what felt like an *hour*, although it couldn't have been more than a few minutes. Noor rolled over in bed and gazed at the ceiling while her phone continued to ring, the back of it making a fart noise as it connected with the table. She didn't even bother to check who was calling—it was probably Ishaan. He had texted that morning and called twice while she was at school and now that he was probably home, he was calling her every fifteen minutes. Well, *let* him suffer. Let them all suffer. She had skipped the TOD/Split meeting and come straight home. That stupid Diya was probably lording it over everyone else and now she could have Ishaan all to herself if she wanted, which she probably did.

Diya *deserved* to be made fun of, Noor thought to herself fiercely. Let her just *try* something now, just *try* and Noor would make her life so *miserable*. But try as she might, Noor couldn't whip herself up into the righteous anger she needed. She was just tired, but also—okay—at the back of her head, slightly relieved. Now everyone knew about the awful thing that Ammi had done and now everyone could just leave her alone about it.

Ring-brrt-ring-brrt, went her phone on the table again. Oh my god, what did he *want*?

'Noor?' said Ishaan's voice. She jumped. Had he turned on her phone and managed to answer it as well?

'Noor, I *know* you're here.'

She reached for her phone and gazed at it. The screen was deceptively black. Maybe he was, like, a super hacker. How much about her did he *know* already? Her mind went to some photos she had taken of herself—just for fun, of course—in front of the bathroom mirror with just a bra and panties on. She thought she was being all fashion model-y, and had even filtered it with some artful bubbles covering up most of her nakedness but you could still see *some* stuff. Had he seen them? She was totally not ready for him to see her without her clothes on.

There was a knock on the door and Noor whirled around to face it.

'Are you decent? Because I'm coming in.' And then, there he was in her room, and she only in a tank top and shorts and no bra on. She quickly crossed her arms over her chest.

'Hey,' he said, not-so-subtly eyeballing her legs. 'You look . . . nice.'

You look nice? That was all he was going to say?

'Um . . .' she managed, and tried once more to summon up being mad at him and the world, but *man*, he looked so *cute* there in his T-shirt and jeans, grinning at her and totally obviously checking her out. *Thank God I shaved my legs*, she thought, and then, because it wouldn't do to give him such a warm welcome, 'What are you *doing* here?'

He looked pleased with himself at the effect he was obviously having on her. 'I'm sorry for just barging in,' he said, not sounding all that sorry. 'But you weren't picking up my calls.'

'Yeah,' said Noor. 'Forty-three missed calls is a bit excessive though, wouldn't you say?'

'I was a desperate man,' he said, and she smirked a little at him calling himself a 'man', like, *as if.* She was still light years away from being a woman, no matter what her body did every month and, right now, his smooth face and kind eyes looking at her through his glasses made him look very boyish.

'And then, I looked for you at school and you weren't there either.'

'I went to school today,' she protested. 'You probably just didn't see me.' *Because I spent all day hiding when I wasn't in class.*

'I even asked your friend where you were and she looked at me weirdly.'

'Um, wow,' said Noor, her brain panicking at the idea of this world and that world colliding. 'Which friend?'

'The kinda plump one?' *Sonum.* 'She seemed easier to talk to than the others.'

'Was she?' asked Noor, already knowing the answer.

'Not really. She was kinda bitchy, actually.'

Noor laughed unexpectedly. She couldn't help it. It just felt really liberating to have someone outside the Group to talk about the Group with. 'How was she bitchy?'

'She gave me this *look* like I smelled or something and then she looked me up and down. And the tall, thin one—'

'Armana.'

'Right. Armana. She was standing a little away from us with that one with the pink hair—'

'Natasha. And she doesn't have pink *hair*, she has pink *highlights.*'

'Right. That. Anyway, so Arunima goes—'

'Armana!' said Noor, giggling. Imagine Armana called *Arunima*. Part of her popular-girl thing was wrapped up in her name.

'Sorry, my bad, Anuradha goes, "Hurry it up, Sonum! What's *taking* so long?" and the fat chick turns to me and says, "*I don't know where Noor is and I don't care either,*" and I said, "Wow, aren't you guys friends?" and *then,* she engaged some lever in her brain to start up super-bitchy mode or something and looked at me—and her eyes got all tiny—and said, "Well, maybe if Noor hadn't *lied* to us about having a boyfriend." Then Anukriti said, "Sonum, we're leaving," and began to walk off and Sonum ran off behind them like she had cracked a whip.' He moved his hand in a whip-cracking motion. 'Crack!'

'I didn't *lie* to them,' Noor said, outraged. 'I just had a lot of shit going on and I didn't want to tell them everything. Can't I have my own life once in a while?'

'I know you have a lot of shit going on.' Ishaan looked at her so sympathetically that she walked towards him and let him wrap his arms around her. She rested her head against his chest and felt his heart thump against her ear. This was the most contact they had had but it felt safe and comfortable, even though she wasn't wearing a bra—it didn't feel *sexual* at all.

And of course, this was the moment the HOC walked in.

Oh, the drama.

First, there was a lot of Quavery Voice, and the HOC stretched out one withered hand, indicating that she'd had a big shock and needed to sit down. Ishaan complied, leading her to the bed while Noor snatched up a bathrobe and draped it around herself so she could feel more in command of the situation. No one could feel one hundred per cent composed when they weren't wearing a bra.

Then, there was a 'Gudiya? Gudiyaaaaa,' as if the HOC was going into the light, which Noor silently encouraged her to. *Step right up, step towards the light, God is waiting, no refunds, no discounts, just go straight through.*

Noor sighed, rolled her eyes and blew upwards towards her bangs dramatically. 'Daadi, this is my friend, Ishaan.'

Through all this, the HOC's eyes gleamed—positively *glinted*. She looked like Gollum in *The Lord of the Rings* gloating over his precious, except in this case, her precious was the fact that she could finally show that Noor was as bad as her absconding mother. QED! You made a mistake, Son!

'A friend? Fine friends you have, to come up straight to your *bedroom*, with the door closed, while you wear God-knows-what.' She could have been harsher but Noor suspected she was toning it down a bit because Ishaan was there. Wouldn't want this boy—obviously from a good family—to think any less of her just because of a wayward granddaughter.

'It's my fault, Aunty,' said Ishaan, surprisingly. He was using all this courtly Hindi too, lots of poetical flourishes and long words—it was practically *Sanskrit*. Noor looked at him goggle-eyed. She wouldn't have assumed a boy from Bombay could use the same words her grandmother did.

'I was worried about Noor because she looked sad in school today and so when I couldn't get through to her on the phone, I lost all sense and came running here. Noor didn't know any of this, I promise.' Ishaan was sitting next to the HOC while he said all this and he reached out and took her hand between his. 'Noor is a *good* girl, Aunty, always so happy and smart and clever, so when we—I, her friends—see her looking sad, obviously, we get worried.'

The HOC was now looking at Noor suspiciously to ferret out the 'good', 'happy', 'smart' and 'clever' version of her from underneath her sullen home-face. While she was still speechless, Ishaan went on to add, 'And *obviously*, I didn't mind my manners. I should have waited while you called her. But I was anxious to see her.'

'What is your relationship with my granddaughter?' asked the HOC, taking back her hand and trying to look stern. But she was won over, Noor could tell. Even the HOC, with her grim old ways, was looking a little dewy-eyed in the face of Ishaan's cuteness, his *niceness*. His nice-cuteness. Noor tried very hard not to smile and bit the corner of her lip, making it look like she was scowling instead.

'Me? I'm a new friend, Aunty,' Ishaan turned his full face on her, making his eyes very big. 'I have just moved here because my parents are getting divorced,' (The HOC made a motion of surprise. They didn't discuss the D-word openly in their home.) 'and Noor has been so kind and helpful to me. You know, it's the hardest on the children.'

He looked sad and the HOC was compelled to say, 'I know, beta, it's so sad. Now, in my time, no one got divorced at all and our children were all raised in one household. You know, I blame this on women who go and get jobs outside the house.'

Ishaan didn't rise to the bait, just said, 'Mmm hmm, mm hmm' and nodded as if he agreed and that was it! The HOC just left saying, 'I'll send some snacks up while you two talk.' Noor gazed flabbergasted and open mouthed at the doorway—which had been left wide open, propped by the doorstop, in the HOC's wake.

'Wow,' she said slowly.

'Wow what?' he grinned, now lounging against her Tweety Bird cushion.

Noor sat down next to him and said, 'You know what, wow. I can't believe she just *left* instead of creating some big scene.'

'Eh,' Ishaan made a waving motion with his hand. 'Old people are easy.'

'No, but *seriously*. She has been giving me a hard time about *everything* and you just go on about how smart and clever I am—nice work, by the way—and she eats it up!'

'You are, though.' Ishaan pushed a piece of hair back from her face and Noor felt her cheeks grow hot. 'You're really smart and nice and clever.'

For a minute, neither of them said anything, just

smiled at each other in the satisfied way that comes with knowing you're with exactly the person you want to be with and then, Noor said, 'And you didn't even get mad when she was all like, "Oh, the reason people get divorced is because women work." Ugh, that would have made me, like, *hopping*.'

'Well,' said Ishaan, picking up Noor's hand and tracing his forefinger down her life line. 'The first time my mother had an affair was when she went back to work after not working for fifteen years.'

Noor didn't know what to say, so she squeezed his hand to indicate she was listening. He smiled his half-smile and said, 'She and my dad made up after he found out about the affair. Then, they decided to have a second honeymoon, and then she came back and had another affair.'

'Oh God.'

'Yeah, and it always ended the same way. My mother has all these little tells, you know? Like, she'd suddenly start humming while she pottered around the house. And she's not a potterer by nature—she has chore days, and every day has a designated thing that needs to be done—but when she'd be cheating on my dad, she'd float around, dusting random things and humming. It was so obvious. It's like we got a quota of happiness and she was using it all up—because the happier she got, the more tense me and my dad were.'

Did Ammi have a 'tell' before she went away? If anything, the fights increased. For a few days, they'd have calm, so much calm that Noor could breathe again, go back to daydreaming about the next family vacation they'd take when her parents would be loving and kind to each other, when they'd laugh and walk through busy markets looking the epitome of a happy family. And that's when her parents had started fighting again—ironically, about Noor's passport, which hadn't been renewed and which each parent blamed the other for, for not being on top of.

The Great Passport Fight had followed the massive Why Do I Have To Take Care Of Everything Around Here fight and was chased soon after by the epic You Never Wanted Me To Follow My Dreams fight. That last one was the one that ended in Ammi crying and Noor had been shocked, as you always are when you catch a parent in tears. Parents aren't supposed to cry. They're supposed to be the strong, stalwart ones who never shed a tear and are always there for comfort and cuddles, much like life-size teddy bears. Noor felt awkward and uncomfortable in the presence of her mother's tears, like she was supposed to offer comfort but couldn't bring herself to. It was all wrong—*she* was the child; she was the one who wept.

How strange life is, thought Noor. *If Ammi hadn't left, I'd still be having those conversations. At least, now I can sleep at night a little. If Ammi hadn't left, I'd never have met Ishaan.*

She smiled brilliantly at Ishaan then.

'What?' he asked, also smiling.

'I was just thinking about that old saying, "Every cloud has a silver lining".'

'Yeah? What about it?'

'It's sort of like,' Noor licked her lips and looked down. 'It's like *you're* my silver lining.'

She expected him to look blown away by this admission—

she certainly hadn't meant to make it—but he looked a little worried.

'What?' she asked. 'Too soon? Are you, like, totally freaked out?'

'Noooo,' he took her hand and looked at her and she knew he was going to say something that would make her sad. She knew that look. She was intimate with that look thanks to her parents, the expression that said 'Oh my God, I really don't want to tell you this but—' The 'but' was about to be dropped.

'I also came over to tell you I won't be in school tomorrow. I'm going to court with my mother. My dad's going to be there as well. It's this custody thing.'

Noor knew he was telling her something that she should be upset about but because she didn't know how the whole custody thing worked, she couldn't figure out which bit of the sentence to worry about.

'What happens then?' she asked him.

'Well, the judge is supposed to also ask me whom I want to live with.'

A cold feeling filled Noor's heart and she waited for him to go on.

'I can't do it, Noor,' He looked really anguished. 'I can't live with my mother anymore. She doesn't care about me— I *know* she doesn't. She's just using me to get back at my dad. I . . . I miss him.'

But what about meeeeee, asked Noor's heart. But Noor's brain could see the expression on Ishaan's face, his eyes so sad, his mouth turned downwards. If she had been given a choice, she'd have lived with her mother. At least, she thought she would have. Maybe not with Sunny Uncle, but if it were just her and her mother.

'Okay,' she said, sounding a bit strangled.

Ishaan took her hand, still not smiling, and kissed her palm. 'You are the best thing that has happened to me in the longest time. But I need to go home, Noor. My dad needs me. In the beginning, I missed my school, my friends, my *life*, you know? But now, it's just my dad. I have to go be with him.'

'What about your mother?' asked Noor. She couldn't fathom a world where both parents didn't dote on their son or daughter. It was too weird. Parents loved you more than anyone else did. That's just how things were. But Ishaan sounded so *sure* of himself, like it was a matter of fact that his mother didn't love him. *Could* mothers not love their children? Did Ammi not love her as much as Noor thought she did?

'My mother is a piece of work,' said Ishaan, huffing. 'She cares about the people she meets, the parties she goes to, the clothes she wears. She's back home, living with her parents, and doesn't have to lift a finger. The only time she looks at me is to see if I'm dressed well. That's all she cares about.'

'Oh Ishaan, I'm sure that's not true!' said Noor before she could help herself, but he didn't look like he minded.

'I know it's hard for you to understand, Noor,' he said. 'But trust me. My mother doesn't like being a mother.'

'I don't think my mother did either,' said Noor, frowning.

'I don't know,' Ishaan was smiling again, lifting a piece of her hair and twirling it around his finger, 'it sounds like—whenever you've spoken about her—like you guys were super tight. Kind of like me and my dad. That kind of thing doesn't go away.'

And then he kissed her—and she kissed him back—and all thoughts of abandoning mothers and court cases were swept away.

The phone was ringing again.

Noor, who had just finished her homework, reached for it where it was sitting to charge by her bedside table. She thought it might be Ishaan again, but he had just left. Just left after an afternoon where he had kissed her till her ears rung and her head felt light. She didn't think it was possible to be kissed like that, kissed so deeply, his hand up in her hair, kneading the back of her skull, his other hand on her chin, drawing her lips closer towards him. She closed her eyes and gave a pleasurable shiver.

But it wasn't Ishaan. The number said 'Armana Cell' and when Noor picked up, half afraid, she heard the familiar static in the background that indicated that she was on the Group's evening con-call.

Since their fight, she hadn't, of course, been expected to be included in the evening call at all. She missed them all so fiercely, but she had also been really angry. Maybe she still was a little angry. It would explain why she said hello in her most frosty tone.

'She's on,' said Armana, and there was silence for a bit, everyone breathing. Noor could hear Sonum's stuffy nose—Sonum always had some sort of allergy—and the faint sound of traffic from Sanvi's walk in the park and the tinny music coming from Natasha's end of the phone call.

'So go on, guys, say what you had to,' said Sanvi.

Sonum: 'Why should we apologize?'

Sanvi: 'Because you've been treating her really shittily.'

Sonum: 'I have *not!*'

Sanvi: 'Yes, you have. Not just you. Also Natasha and Armana.'

Armana: 'Since when did you become Mother Teresa?'

Sanvi: 'I'm not. I haven't. I'm just tired of the way you guys judge us if we choose not to date your football players with their collective one brain cell.'

Natasha: 'Hey!'

Sanvi: 'I'm sorry, but you guys have been giving me a hard time for dating Aryan from the beginning. I took it because I got that you didn't understand us.'

Armana: 'Oh, yes, the mysteries of the Sanvi–Aryan hook-up is something I stay up at night thinking about.'

Sanvi: 'Why do you got to be such a *bitch*, Armana?'

Armana: 'WHAT did you say to me?'

Natasha: 'There's no need to call anyone names, Sanvi.'

Sanvi: 'You're all hearing how rude she's being to me about my boyfriend, right?'

~silence~

Sonum: 'I must say, Sanvi, I really think that you are—'

Noor: 'Sanvi's right. Why *are* you so mean about her relationship, Armana?'

Armana: 'Oh, look who's decided to speak up *now!*'

Noor: 'Listen guys, there's a lot going on in my life right now. Maybe I should have told you about it all sooner. But I kinda felt like holding on to it. Like it wouldn't be real if I didn't spell it out.'

Natasha: '*What* Noor? *What* exactly is this big crisis that's going on in your life?'

Sonum: 'Maybe her boyfriend dumped her.'

Noor: 'At least I *have* a boyfriend, Sonum. Where's yours?'

Armana: 'Hah! Good point!'

Noor: 'The big crisis that's going on in my life is . . .' (drawing a deep breath) 'My parents are getting divorced.'

~silence~

Natasha: 'Are you serious? Oh, Noor! That is so sad!'

Armana: 'Roxy showed your dad the door?'

Noor (managing to laugh a little): 'The other way round, actually: my mother has absconded with her childhood sweetheart. A dude called Sunil Doda.'

Natasha: 'OH. MY. GOD.'

Armana: 'Have you googled him? Someone, google him!'

Noor: 'I've googled him! He's . . . unremarkable.'

Natasha: 'That sucks. I'm so sorry, Noorlette.'

Noor: 'Thanks. And that's how I met Ishaan—um, my boyfriend—at this after-school kids-of-divorce club Saras set up.'

Armana: 'That is, like, *seriously* romantic. Speaking of, Reansh has been acting very strange lately . . .'

And they were off! The conversation moved swiftly from Noor's parents to Reansh's mysterious, suddenly distant behaviour and then to how Natasha was invited to Prateek's cousin's wedding with him and what she should wear. Sonum, reeling from her snub earlier, was uncharacteristically quiet.

When the conversation ended, Noor's phone rang again and it was Sanvi.

'I'm sorry to hear about your parents,' she said quietly, and Noor knew she meant it.

'I'm sorry Armana was so rude about Aryan,' she offered in return. 'But now that everything is back to normal, I guess we can discuss it?'

Sanvi laughed softly, 'I don't know if I want to. I've been feeling more and more like I'm drifting away from the Group, not just because of Aryan, but just because everyone is so *different* from me. I've met some cool people through Aryan . . . I might hang out with them more.'

'What does this mean?' asked Noor. 'Are you dumping us?' She half laughed at the idea but Sanvi was quiet.

'Maybe? Maybe I am. Not *you*. I think you and I have become closer these last few months, right?'

'Yup.'

'Yeah, so we'll still be friends, but this Group thing, I don't know if it's for me, Noor.'

A few months ago, Noor would have been deeply distressed by this news, but she now knew that sometimes, you just had to cut your losses and move on. That was the idea. *Just keep swimming*, as the little blue fish had said in *Finding Nemo*, a movie she had loved as a kid. *Just keep swimming*.

'I guess if it feels like the right choice to you,' she said to Sanvi, and she heard Sanvi let out her breath as if she had been holding it. And Noor was glad she was there for her friend.

'Hey, and maybe you and Ishaan and Aryan and I can all go out sometime?' asked Sanvi, and Noor said, 'Totally!'

It all sounded like it was going to work out after all.

9

So, this was Ishaan's house. Noor was in his grandparents' car, which had picked her up and brought her over. Ishaan's mother was having a 'lunch' and she had allowed Ishaan to bring a friend.

'Normally, I wouldn't even care,' he had told Noor on the phone. 'But it'll be good food—at least her menu planning is decent—and we'll have a chance to hang out.'

Noor had to admit she was super curious about Ishaan's mysterious house. The Manipulative Grandparents. The Evil Mother Who Only Loved Parties. It was like something out of a movie.

'What should I wear?' she asked him and he said, 'Oh, anything.' So she asked Sanvi instead. Sanvi was turning into someone she talked to every day, sometimes for hours. They'd stay up late IMing, but not constantly, more like whenever one of them thought of something the other one would find interesting.

'Proper, but casual. Like, you don't want to walk around with a low-cut top or anything but you don't want to look like a nun,' was her sage advice and bearing that in mind,

163

Noor had chosen a white shift dress that she had always loved—with beaded embroidery across the top—and low heels. Nobody had been home when Ishaan's driver came to pick her up, which in itself was odd. Noor wasn't used to leaving the house without asking for permission, but so many strange things had become normal. So she had just sent a text to her father saying she was going out with a friend for lunch and that her friend would drop her home. Careful avoidance of any pronouns to indicate gender. The HOC was out at some large gathering that old people did every now and then, where they'd eat a lot of food and bitch about their families and lament their lots in life.

Ishaan's grandfather had some high-up post in the government and so they had been allotted a pretty home in the middle of Delhi, with enough space for a long, loopy driveway that led to the front porch, a manicured lawn next to it and huge white columns holding up the roof so you could get out of your car un-inconvenienced by the weather.

Ishaan must have been watching out for her because almost as soon as the car stopped, he was outside, smiling at her, opening the door to let her out. And she put one heel out, feeling more and more like this was a movie and there was a camera slow-panning up her leg to her dress and then up to her face. She was glad she had decided to dress up, when she saw that he was wearing a rather nice checked shirt tucked into skinny jeans and new purple sneakers. She smiled when she saw the shoes.

'What?' he asked.

'Nothing! I just never took you for a hipster.'

He laughed. 'This is my mother's idea of men's fashion. I want to keep her sweet so she doesn't put up too much of a fight about the judgement. I mean, I *think* the judge heard what I had to say but she can always battle it out for another two years, just out of spite.' And then, in reaction to Noor's expression, 'Hey, don't worry about it. We'll figure it out. Let's just have a nice time today.'

He took Noor's hand and led her up the stairs. Noor was a little shy of this public hand-holding. The gesture was still so new to her, despite copious amounts of practice and she didn't want all the security guards and the help to notice and judge her. But Ishaan didn't seem to care at all, and hey, it *was* his house and he probably knew best, so she let him guide her down a corridor that could have been a Good Earth store—so full of handicrafts and wall hangings was it—beneath a staircase, and to a room where he knocked on the door and let go of her hand.

'Come in,' said a clipped male voice, and Ishaan opened the door and smiled at Noor encouragingly.

'I wanted you to meet my friend, Noor,' he said to the man inside, an old man, but still clearly someone who commanded respect. In fact, Noor felt herself stand up straighter in his presence. His hair was very white, but still thick, brushed to one side, his moustache lovingly tended. He was sitting behind a very large desk and working at his computer, but when he saw them enter, he stood up as well, a gentlemanly gesture, and crossed the room from behind his desk to shake Noor's hand.

'Welcome, young lady,' he said. 'I hope Ishaan is looking after you.'

She tried to muster up dislike, or even cold contempt for him, but she couldn't. He had a twinkle in his eyes, and his moustache was both intimidating and comforting as it quirked over his mouth. And she knew he could be rigid and unreasonable from whatever Ishaan had said, but he was his *grandfather* and surely that meant Ishaan loved him somewhere deep inside.

'I'm fine, thank you,' she told him, and he dropped her hand and said, 'Splendid!' in that same not-quite-British accent that older civil servants seemed to always have.

Ishaan was making let's-get-out-of-here faces, and so she said, 'Very nice to meet you,' and Ishaan led her out of there and under the staircase again, where she was surprised to find someone had placed two armchairs, almost as if this was a regular meeting place for people in this house.

'Sorry,' said Ishaan, 'he likes to meet everyone who comes to this house. It's so he feels included. He doesn't attend most of the parties, so this is his way of letting people who come here know whose house it is. As if we'd forget.'

Noor sat down on one of the armchairs. It was very comfortable but also very white, and by years of habit, she sat just on the edge of it so she wouldn't accidentally get it dirty. *Things* could just *happen* to a white surface. It was like the white attracted all sorts of other colours so it wouldn't have to be lonely and blank by itself.

'Can I have a glass of water?' she asked him.

'Oh, sure! Of course!' Ishaan looked a bit stricken at having forgotten this basic courtesy. 'I can even do one better and get you a glass of really good strawberry-

and-basil lemonade but that would mean meeting my mother.'

Noor tried to look like this decision was totally not up to her and she didn't care one way or another and, in fact, she'd just sit here on this white sofa if that was where he wanted her to sit. *Completely* chill.

Ishaan fiddled with a couple of threads on his wrist. On closer inspection, Noor realized they weren't just random threads, they were threads woven together in a deliberate pattern—black and orange, braided, in and out.

'Is that a *friend*ship band?' she asked.

'Oh, yeah.' Ishaan looked down at it as if he had forgotten what he was playing with. 'It's from, um . . . it's from a Split meeting. The last time we met, we made friendship bands.'

'Oh,' said Noor, her jaw hurting from setting it so tight. 'Sounds super lame.'

'It *was*, but it was Saraswati's idea and you know she doesn't say much, so we thought we should encourage her.'

She *did* know Saraswati didn't say much. She had been growing fond of Saraswati, who asked for affection, totally unlike the more voluble Ankur. Saraswati had a way of creeping up on you and curling around you, like a cat you tried to shoo away but ultimately let settle on your lap like it was doing you a great favour.

'We missed you though,' Ishaan said. 'It wasn't the same without you there.'

'I bet Diya didn't miss me,' muttered Noor.

'Even Diya. She felt bad about what she said to you. She had a long chat with Saras about her, quote, unquote, *anger* issues.'

'And what did Saras say to that? Did she hear about what happened at the party?'

'Sorta,' Ishaan settled himself on the floor, cross-legged at her feet. 'I mean, I didn't want to say anything and you could tell that Diya didn't but the kids were full of it.'

Noor smiled. 'I like the way you said "the kids", like they belong to you too.'

'Yeah,' Ishaan smiled back at her, 'they feel a bit like they belong to me, you know? I guess I realized I'm going to miss more than you when I leave.'

She looked at him, full of sorrow.

'I know,' he said. 'Don't say it. So, anyway, Saras was all like, "Do *you* think you behaved in a compassionate and responsible way, Diya?" and that really got to her—you know how she's all about responsibility. And then she started crying.'

'*Crying?*'

'Crying. And she was like, "Oh, I'm such a *horrible* person", and then we all had to be, "No, you're not".'

'She is, though.'

'Noor, give her a break. Anyway, then she had a long chat while we were making friendship bracelets and she decided to write you a letter.'

'A *letter?* Like she doesn't see me at school every day.'

'Well, Saras said that sometimes it's easier to say what's in your heart if you don't have to gauge what a person is feeling the entire time. The burden of their feelings shouldn't take away from what you want to say, and so many times, you know, we begin saying something and we see how someone reacts and that sort of changes the *tone* of what we're saying, you know?'

'Wow. Deep.'

'Saras is pretty deep, sometimes.'

They sat in silence for a bit. And then, 'Okay, I think we've put it off long enough. Come and meet the monster.'

The 'monster' was a slight, still-lovely woman, dressed in a cream shirt and spotless white pants, looking as though she had never had an unsightly stain in her life. Her perfectly done hair was perfectly coloured, but not that cheap orange that most people seemed to choose or even a brittle blonde. Her copper highlights worked with the rest of her hair, giving her the appearance of someone who was rich—but not money-rich, more like how you'd describe a dessert. *Rich. Full of butter. Dark chocolate.*

She had been talking to some people when they entered, and even though Noor was fairly sure she had seen them, she finished her sentence before shaking back her glossy head and extending a thin hand, full of sinews—and with a huge cocktail ring on the middle finger—to Ishaan. *This is what Armana will be when she grows up,* realized Noor with a thrill.

'*There* you are! I was just telling everyone that you had a guest you were entertaining as well,' said Ishaan's mother, while Noor tried desperately to figure out how to address her. 'Aunty' was what she normally went with for friends' mothers but this was no aunty. This was some glamorous movie-star-type figure, with gestures that seemed so alien to any concept of an aunty. Aunties wore housecoats or loose nighties all day on Sunday and cooked with vast amounts of chilli or haldi and called you 'beta'. Noor knew instinctively that this woman would never call her 'beta', had probably never used the word 'beta' in her life.

Luckily, Ishaan took it out of her hands. 'Noor, this is my mother, Sharmila. Ma, Noor.'

'Hello,' squeaked Noor. Was it better to have an absent mother or one who was absent even when she was standing right there in front of you?

'Call me Sharmila,' said Sharmila, even though Noor had not volunteered anything else. Noor got the sense that she could see into Noor's inner soul, and whatever she saw, she was amused by. 'Get her a drink, Ishaan. There's some lemonade over there. Some Sprite in the fridge if you like that ghastly stuff.'

'No,' said Noor, feeling about twelve. 'Lemonade is fine.'

'Sure? Because we have both. Okay, Ishaan, get her a drink, and Noor, you come and sit by us.'

The gaggle of women who had stopped talking when the two came in began to move each other along the sofa and opened up a spot for her right in the centre. Noor cautiously sat down, and looked over at Ishaan, who had decided they needed more ice and had left her all alone in the wilderness.

'So,' said one of them, who *did* have the brittle blonde hair, 'are you Ishaan's girlfriend?'

'Hai,' said another, sipping her wine almost angrily. 'If Ishaan has a girlfriend, how old does that make us?'

'*Too* old to have this conversation,' said the third, who

looked more like the adults Noor recognized, dressed in a long cotton kaftan and with short salt-and-pepper hair. 'You leave the poor thing alone.' She had a deep, husky voice and she leaned over and said to Noor conspiratorially, 'You see, dear, we're all school friends, and we've run out of things to talk about over the years, so we pick on our children's friends.'

School friends! She would never be like that, the *Group* would never be like that, but as she glanced around her, she noticed the Sonum (the blonde, wearing almost exactly the same thing as Ishaan's mother, but contriving to look old in her imitation), the Natasha (the angry wine-drinker), which meant that the grey-haired lady was *her*. How funny.

'But are you Ishaan's girlfriend?' asked Old Sonum, and Noor could bet she had a son of her own, and whose girlfriend she was comparing to Noor right now in her head.

'Um,' she glanced at Sharmila, who was playing with the ring on her finger and looking even more amused.

'Of course she is, see her blushing,' said Old Natasha, who was helping herself to more wine. 'How is *your* son though, Babita?'

Babita/Sonum immediately sat up a little straighter. 'Good!' she said. 'He's good. So many friends, so popular, I never see him.'

'Any special people in his life?' asked Old Natasha, with a look of deep meaning, but Babita just fluttered and said no, there weren't.

'Babita's son is gay,' said Old Noor, 'and she's terrified that means she's a bad mother. Do you have any gay friends, Noor?'

'Hema!' said Babita in a tone of deep shock, and Noor, whose eyes had opened very wide at Hema/Noor's last sentence, managed to pull herself together enough to say, 'No, no gay friends.'

'You see? My poor Yudh,' said Babita/Sonum sniffing, pulling out a hanky from her rose-shaped clutch. 'So lonely. But maybe,' hopefully, 'he only *thinks* he's gay.'

Before Noor could say anything to that, Ishaan came back and offered her a glass. She sipped it gratefully—it *was* very good, all tart with the strawberries and lemon and still sweet.

'Ishoo, how's school?' asked Babita/Sonum, glad for the subject to be off her son.

'Eh, school's school,' said 'Ishoo'. 'Noor, you want to go see my room?'

Noor nodded and stood up and wondered that Ishaan's mother didn't say anything to this, didn't even flash worried eyes at Ishaan or remind him to leave the door open.

This must be what it's like to be a son, she thought to herself, *no one actually tells you what to do.*

'Come down later for lunch,' said Sharmila, and waved the tips of her fingers at them. Noor said, 'Bye,' softly, and Old Noor was the only one who looked up—looked up and winked. 'Be good,' said Old Noor but only Noor heard her, which seemed appropriate.

'It's been a great afternoon,' said Noor, getting up with a sigh. They had been lying on Ishaan's bed but mostly just talking. Some kissing. Some touching. But the bulk of their afternoon had been talk—'what's your favourite' and 'how old were you when' and 'what do you think of' and so on and so forth, till Noor's throat was hoarse from saying so much, and her eyes, when she stood up, had to refocus from gazing into Ishaan's for the last two hours.

'A strange afternoon too, though, right?' said Ishaan, coming up behind her and putting his hands on her shoulders. 'Sorry about the old bats. They've been drinking and they get mouthy when they drink.'

'They weren't so bad,' said Noor. She decided not to tell Ishaan about the weird feeling she had, like the Group had aged, and how all groups were really the same. Ishaan didn't think very highly of her friends to begin with, and, while recently they *had* been pretty shitty, only Noor got to criticize them. No boyfriend did, no matter how nice he was.

'Noor,' said Ishaan, now facing her.

'Yes?' she grinned at him, expecting him to joke about something, but he looked quite serious.

'I wanted to give you this,' he reached into his back pocket and pulled out a friendship band, this one picked out in purple and silver.

'Aww, you made me a friendship band? That's so sweet. And dorky.' She stuck her tongue out at him. 'But mostly sweet. Put it on?'

He took her wrist and tied it on and said, 'There,' and she looked down at it. 'Perfect! I love it. Thank you.'

'I love *you*.'

Silence, while the words entered her brain, where it began a yell of joy, until she subdued it.

He *loved* her. Did she love him? What *was* love? Could love be these endless afternoons with someone you liked so, so, *so* much, the thought of them making your heart burst? And could this love be separated from the love that made people leave their families and cause pain and heartache? Would all love paths lead to the same eventual highway?

'Oka-aay,' she said, stalling for time.

He looked hurt. 'Don't you feel the same way? I thought you did.'

'I . . .' she looked up to the ceiling for inspiration but none was forthcoming. 'I don't know how I feel.'

'I think you do, though,' he said, now smiling, and reaching out to link her fingers through his.

She pulled away. 'I *don't*, though.' Her throat was closing. If she didn't give him the correct answer, she'd lose him too, but somewhere inside her, she felt like if she gave in on this, she'd be giving in on everything.

'What are you confused about?'

'This.' She waved at the space between them. 'The two of us. I mean, all this while, I've been thinking that love is sort of stupid, right? That's why my mother hurt my father. That's *how* your mother hurt your father. Isn't that pretty awful? Wouldn't it be better to be without?'

'Noor,' he said, heavily, and seemed about to go on, when he stopped himself.

'And that's your final answer?' he asked, leaning against the door, his arms crossed.

'I'm really sorry. I wish I could tell you something else, but this is how I *feel*,' said Noor, almost wailing. Her lovely afternoon had shattered and fallen all over the carpet.

'You're really stupid,' he said, sighing deeply.

She felt a bit stupid too. Ugh, see, this totally proved that love made everything so *hard*.

Noor had just exited class, when she saw the crowd around the girl's toilet on their floor. She really had to pee, so she fought her way through the tangle of girls standing around, whispering. She heard people say, 'Just out of the blue!' and 'Armana' and then as she moved through them, she noticed that their voices got hushed as they saw her, and their eyes avid—no, not with sympathy, this was something more brutish, something that wanted feeding—sparkling at her.

'Let her go through, she's her best friend after all,' said a voice, and she looked up and saw Diya with her friends. Noor made stern eye contact and Diya held her gaze unashamed. Still, Noor felt a frisson of pleasure through her worry at the words 'her best friend'. It never failed to gratify her, her association with the Group. It made her special, it made her stand out and, best of all, it marked her with a sort of members-only badge, part of an exclusive club that no one else belonged to. Feeling very righteous and also very curious, she pushed open the door, which stuck, because Sonum was on the other side, guarding it.

'I *said* it's occupied,' said Sonum loudly, and then, seeing Noor, 'Oh, it's you.'

'Yes, it's me,' said Noor. 'What's going on?'

Was that really Armana there sitting on the toilet lid,

weeping as if her heart would break? Natasha hovered near her, handing her tissues and patting her back.

'Armana?' said Noor. 'What happened? What's going on?' And then, because she *did* really have to use the bathroom, she went into another stall, peed quickly and emerged again, facing them in the mirror as she washed her hands. Armana had begun a renewed bout of weeping when she spotted Noor and Noor wanted to shake some sense out of her, out of *any* of them really. Her curiosity was replaced by a more urgent need to figure out what was wrong. She even felt a little stab of guilt at herself for wanting to be part of the drama in the first place.

Noor crossed the room and squatted down next to Armana, trying not to inhale the loo smells and then she said gently, 'Armana? Talk to me.'

'He *left* me!' wailed Armana.

'Who left you?' asked Noor, thinking, *It's got to be her dad. Why else would she be so upset? Well, at least we can be in the same boat. Divorce buddies! Maybe Armana and I will become closer now that we have that in common.* She had this whole fantasy planned out in her head, even thinking about how she'd spend the night more at Armana's and the two of them would be more intimate than they had ever been and it wasn't going to be so bad for her now because there'd be Armana! And with Armana in the same situation as her, even divorce could be cool.

It came as quite a shock then, when Armana sniffled and said, 'Reansh! He left *me*!' And this time, she put the emphasis on 'me' because really, who wouldn't be surprised at Reansh leaving Armana the Golden? Everyone wanted to be with her or *be* her, she had once said, laughing, but the Group had known it was true.

Noor looked up and caught Natasha's eye, like, *is this a thing?* And Natasha nodded solemnly, *it's a thing.*

'Um,' said Noor. 'Okay. What happened? Maybe it was a misunderstanding.'

Armana looked up, and even with her tear-swollen eyes, managed to throw Noor a look of scorn. 'It wasn't a misunderstanding,' she said. 'He decided he'd rather be with that . . . that *whore!*'

'*Who?*' Noor was dying now. *Dying.* If someone didn't tell her what was going on, she would explode.

The story was this (told with Armana's sniffles, Natasha's hushed-voice-of-gravity adopted for the occasion and Sonum's interjections of 'ugh, he's *so not worth it*' in the background as she continued to guard the door).

Reansh had been acting weird lately. ('Define weird.' 'Like, he wasn't replying to my texts for a day at a time, which, normally, he'd reply to immediately. He'd even get really angry if I didn't write back as soon as he sent a message, which I thought was annoying, but now . . .') He not only didn't reply to texts as soon as they were sent, his IM showed him as always offline, or when he *was* online, because he *had* to be—how could he go so long without the Internet?—his status was set to 'Away'. At some point in the last week, he had set his status update on Facebook to lyrics from 'With Or Without You', a song by a band they all listened to or pretended to listen to, despite the fact that it was old, because of the lead singer, a man called Bono, who wore dark glasses and crooned about love.

Armana had thought the fact that he had updated his status at *all* was fishy ('He doesn't talk to me for a week, like, barely making eye contact at school, and then he updates his Facebook, when he *knows* I can see it.') and that particular status was fishier still. ('You give it all but I want more? Like, what is *that*, even?') But she had refrained from commenting on it or even liking it, though she hovered over it obsessively for a few hours to see if he would react to any of the comments posted, mostly variations of: 'bro, u ok bro?' Reansh had replied with an unsatisfactory smiley face, but that night he had sent a message to Armana on Facebook saying, 'Hey, u up? We need to talk.'

('We need to talk is never good.' 'Yeah, but I didn't think he meant, like, *need to talk*-need to talk. We were great! Besides, I hadn't done anything wrong. I thought he wanted to apologize for being missing for the last week.') So Armana had gone in, preparing to be stern but ultimately forgiving, because she 'really, really liked' Reansh, and she liked being his girlfriend. Besides, she was *Armana*. What was the worst that could come out of their discussion?

Reansh had fallen in love—with someone else. The girl in question was 'older', seventeen to their sixteen and in class XII. She wasn't even from Delhi and was staying with her local guardians who happened to know Reansh's parents. Shikha and Reansh had struck up a conversation one evening, when her guardians had gone to Reansh's parents for dinner. He had begun by just talking to her, they had swapped numbers and he found himself texting her all day. And that moved on to him calling her at night and the two of them talking for hours. 'It just sort of *happened*,' he told Armana, who was growing more and more shocked as the conversation progressed. Result: he broke up with Armana and today had been the day his new relationship debuted at school.

'Everyone's *looking* at me,' said Armana. 'He could have been more sensitive about my *feelings*.' Privately, Noor recalled how, when Armana had broken up with Anirudh for Reansh, she hadn't even given him the courtesy of a heads-up. She'd just breezed into school, ignored him and made her way to Reansh, all lower-lip-bitey.

'Okay,' said Natasha. 'Now you show the world that you don't give a fuck.' Armana sniffled a bit more, but her tears seemed to have mostly dried up, and there was a listening air about her slumped shoulders. 'Wash your face,' said Natasha. 'And put on some kajal or something, and when we leave this loo, we'll pretend like *you're* the one who dumped *him*.'

'But I *did*,' said Armana. 'Once he told me that he was in love with this Shikha, I was like, "We can no longer be together."'

Once again, Noor's eyes met Natasha's, and they shared a deep and eloquent look that retied the knots of friendship that had frayed between them.

Armana followed their advice and Sonum produced make up from her backpack and, after brushing out her hair and putting on some lip gloss, Armana almost looked like herself again. In fact, she probably looked exactly the same Armana who had been in school yesterday, but her friends knew that there was something subtly different about her, a sense of bad-things-can-happen-to-me-too that meant Armana may not ever be the same Armana again.

'I loved him and I thought he loved me too,' Armana told them later, when she was more fully composed, dry-eyed and smirk-ready to go. *My dad probably thought the same thing,* thought Noor. She wondered at Reansh. How could you promise to be with one person and then not honour that promise anymore?

But the Group had spied on Reansh as he walked through the inner courtyard to get to the other side. He gave them a sideways glance and then immediately looked away. He was making his way to an unprepossessing girl, with lank hair and a round face. She even wore her skirts too long. What could draw *anyone* to this person, let alone Reansh, who was about as Golden as Armana was? Reansh glimmered and she seemed all dowdy and in the shadows. But then, as her friends looked away pointedly, Noor couldn't resist one last glance at them.

Shikha had her hand on his arm and was telling him something—Noor couldn't tell what—but obviously it was a good story because Reansh was laughing really hard and then when he stopped laughing, he looked down at Shikha's drab little face and there was so much affection in his look, even, maybe, *love*, that he didn't look like a forty-year-old pretending to be a teenager anymore. He looked like, well, like a regular person. And Shikha was almost pretty as she glanced at him, delighted at the reaction her story was getting. Armana and Reansh had never looked at each other like that. *My mother and father never looked at each other like that,* thought Noor suddenly, *and maybe everyone needs someone to tell a story to and have them be really happy that YOU'RE there and YOU'RE telling them this story. Like me and Ishaan.*

Like me and Ishaan.

It struck Noor so suddenly that she had to stop, and Sonum ploughed right into her and said, 'Watch it!'

Oh my God, I love Ishaan.

But what about love sucking?

It was still an inconvenient emotion, but Noor had just realized, as people have been doing for generations, and as people will continue to do, that love is not something you have any sort of control over. She could say, 'Love sucks' till the end of time, and point out a zillion examples, and all those examples still wouldn't lessen the fact that she was in love with Ishaan. As soon as she admitted that to herself, her soul let out a huge sigh, like it had been waiting to hear that all this while and now it could go back to doing what it was meant to do, instead of sitting inside the little box that she had made for it.

Ironically, Noor got a 'We need to talk' text that day as well. Unlike Armana, she wasn't optimistic about the results. It wasn't from Ishaan, though. It was from her father, who asked her to stay back after dinner was over.

Surprisingly, the HOC had cleared up superfast and left. Noor suddenly understood that her father, *her father*, had asked his mother to leave so he could talk to her. She felt, all at once, apprehensive and a little shy. She hadn't spoken to her dad, alone, in so long. What would they say?

'Do you want to tell me why you were entertaining a boy in your bedroom the other day?'

Oh. So much for bonding.

'I already explained it to *your mother*. He didn't tell me he was coming over and he sort of surprised me. I wasn't expecting it. It's not like it was planned.'

'Who is this fellow and why does he think he can surprise you here?'

'You know. Obviously, you already have all your facts from the crone!' Oops, that just slipped out, but she had to keep going now, she was too mad to stop. 'Why don't you just ask *her*? Suddenly you care about my opinion?'

'You will speak of my mother with respect!'

'Respect has to be earned! No one tries to speak to *me* with respect!'

'She gave up everything—*everything*—to move here to look after you!'

'Well, I didn't ask her to. I didn't ask for any of this.'

'Newsflash.' Her dad sounded really tired now. 'Neither did I.'

'Dad, she keeps going on and on, saying Muslims are horrible! How can you let her get away with that?'

'She's old . . .'

'Oh yeah, keep saying that. *Keep* saying she's old. I'm part Muslim. Or are you just going to ignore that?'

'Her family lost everything in the Partition, Noor. She saw some ugly things when she was just a little girl. People never recover from that.'

'Ammi would never,' Noor drew in a long shaky breath. 'Ammi would *never* make me live with someone like that.'

'Oh no? Your sainted Ammi left. That's what she did.'

'I wish *you* had been the one who left!'

'So do I!' Dad looked at her almost with hate. Could fathers hate their daughters? Was it allowed, even? Why were her parents insisting on being unlike every single other parent? Her chin wobbling, but her head held high, Noor left the room, only to dissolve into tears as soon as she was out of eyeshot.

This is not happening to me, she thought, *when I wake up in the morning, everything will be okay, and everything will go back to normal and this will all have been a bad dream.*

She knew that wasn't true, but it comforted her to think about it, so she held that happy thought and gazed at Zayn, but somehow even Zayn wasn't making her feel better like he normally could. After a while, she gave up and stayed up late surfing the internet, finally going to sleep at 4 a.m. and almost missed her alarm when it rang three hours later.

10

Noor felt kind of bad for what she had said to her father the night before. She had the uncomfortable feeling that she had hurt his feelings and it wasn't entirely fair. Of course, the stuff about the HOC *had* to be said, the HOC was *horrible*. Except, well, she wasn't being so horrible anymore.

Before Noor could decide what to do, her father poked his head into her room as she was packing up for school and said, 'Noorie, about last night . . .' He looked as awkward as she felt.

'I'm sorry, Dad,' she managed, and his eyes got all teary and, oh God, she was crying *again* and would the tears ever stop? She was squished up against his belly, her face in his chest. He smelled so familiar and *Dad*-like that she cried even more from relief. There was still a port in the storm right here, *right here*, and she hadn't noticed.

As a result of all this crying, Noor missed her bus to school and her father said he'd drop her off. On the way, she fiddled with the radio till she found something that suited her and just as she was relaxing into the music, her father turned it down.

'Hey!' said Noor.

'Sorry but I had to tell you something I never managed to tell you last night.'

They both blushed at the memory of their fight. *In some ways, I'm just like Dad*, thought Noor, turning her face to the window.

'Your grandmother is leaving, Noorie.'

'Leaving? Is this because of what I said? I'm sorry, Dad, I didn't mean it! I was just, like, *angry*, you know.'

'No, no, of course it's not because of you.' He reached out and placed his hand on top of hers. 'She wants to go stay with my brother, your Arjun Chacha, again. Her life is really in Jaipur, Noor, and she misses it, her friends, her home—you know Arjun Chacha lives in the house that we grew up in.'

Noor thought about this—her grandmother leaving everything behind, her friends, her family, her *life* really, to come and look after the two of them. It was kind of sweet. Okay, so her sort of sweet involved being very religious and pouring God down their throats a lot but it was still a nice gesture. Maybe the HOC wasn't an HOC but a loving grandmother after all. Even if you considered that an old person couldn't have *that* much of a social life, it was nice of her. She said as much to her father, who laughed.

'She? She has a roaring social life. Full of friends. They all meet and play cards and compare recipes and whatnot.'

'She must be looking forward to going back to

Arjun Chacha's kids, huh? They always listen to her and everything.'

'Well,' Dad gave her a sideways grin. 'Between you and me, I don't think your cousins are as pliable as she makes them sound. But I think they've known your daadi for so long, they're able to *pretend* like they're listening to everything she says.'

'Oh,' said Noor, considering. Maybe she should've pretended harder.

'I like that you don't pretend to be anyone but who you are,' said her father, as they pulled into the school's driveway. 'I think it makes for a refreshing change. Even though your views don't match hers, I wanted her to know that I've raised an independent thinker.'

Noor was so pleased she couldn't speak. This was perhaps the nicest thing her father had ever said to her. *Imagine*, she thought, *I'm an independent thinker*.

She managed a wave and a smile as she hopped out. 'Have a good day at school!' said her dad and drove away. Noor's heart ballooned again and she let go of the string just a little bit and it went bob-bob-bob all the way up to her throat.

'Now, what is this very important meeting?' asked Noor, trying to joke about it.

Ishaan had sent her a text message saying, 'Meet me in break? Important,' and now here they were, in a tucked-away corner of the football field, hidden by some trees. Frankly, since the whole 'love' thing, when Ishaan had said it and Noor hadn't, she could feel a certain distance between them. Some words couldn't be unsaid, no matter how much you tried. You could open your mouth really wide and try to stuff the words back in, but they'd always hang around on your tongue, refusing to be swallowed and you'd feel the bile they aroused in you just rise up and lie between you and the person you said them to, until you wished you had a time machine and could unsay everything. Undo, undo, undo!

But then, there was the distinctly contradictory flutter of excitement in her belly she felt each time she thought about it. *Ishaan loves me, he LOVES me, Ishaan loves me,* like a classical song with a merry violin, playing over and over again, making her want to skip. She wanted to tell him she felt the same way now, and talk about all her misgivings about it and make him promise, pinky-swear, that he'd never hurt her. But she couldn't find exactly the right words, the balance between passionate and needy. Also, what if he had changed his mind just because she hadn't said it? What if it was too late?

'When do we get to *meet* this famous Ishaan?' asked Armana, with her usual look of this-is-so-funny-YOU-pretending-to-have-a-boyfriend, but Armana had lost some of her power, and Noor didn't feel hurt or slighted as she normally would have, only a little sorry for Armana. Ishaan loved *her* and no one loved Armana. Not that way, anyway. And Noor wanted to hold her and comfort her and tell her there would be someone else soon. Armana must have seen this look on Noor's face because she suddenly got very busy brushing her hair, and shrugged in Noor's direction. '*I* don't care when we meet him. Whateverrrrr.'

'Hey, dreamer,' Ishaan was holding her hand and looking at her, as they both sat on the grass, 'Where are you? Come back to me.' He didn't look upset or angry or anything, and Noor realized with relief that he wasn't there to break up with her. He just looked at her like she was something small and precious and breakable that he couldn't bear to let go of in case he dropped it. She was suddenly conscious of what a nice day it was, slightly overcast with a gentle breeze that made the trees rustle in a friendly way, like the trees in the *Faraway Tree* books that she used to love not that long ago (and secretly still read sometimes). *Wisha wisha wisha.* The grass against her bare shins was prickly but in a nice way, and she pulled at a weed, working at the stem with her fingernail.

'You're seriously pretty, you know?' said Ishaan just then, and all thoughts of the weather flew from her head as her balloony heart threatened to break free of its string and float up, up, up. She blushed and looked down and he tilted her face upwards. She was biting her lip, and he looked around him to make sure no one was looking and kissed her. And she kind of wished they weren't there, not in *school*, so they could go somewhere and she could kiss him back the way she wanted to, *all in*. But there they were, and so she contained herself to just kissing him back a little and then, he dropped her chin but kept looking at her. And she knew it wasn't good news because he wasn't smiling the way he always smiled when they kissed, no matter if it was the first kiss of the evening or the eleventh. He always got this dreamy expression, his eyes blinking, wonderstruck, his mouth spreading into this shy but glorious smile and she loved that about him. Liked. She meant to think *liked*.

'Noor,' he began, then cleared his throat, 'my, um, my dad won the court case.'

Mixed emotions running through her brain. Why was this so confusing? Focus, Noor, focus. *Okay, so I'm really happy that he gets to be with his dad, he WANTS to be with his dad, but this means he's moving back to Bombay and I'm really sad and can I be happy for HIM and sad for ME at the same time? I think my head is going to explode.*

'It doesn't have to be the end of us, Noor.'

She tried to talk, realized she was about to cry. 'How?' she managed.

'Bombay and Delhi are the two most connected cities in India. I'll be here a *lot*. My mother insists on a weekend a month, at least. And I'll come for longer to see you.'

'I wish,' she choked. 'I wish things were different *now*.'

'I know. But I'm almost seventeen, and next year I'll be eighteen and then no one gets custody of me. I can do what I want.'

Noor shredded the flower she was holding into bits. 'I hate that we can't decide now. I hate that we have to listen to adults all the time, when it's the adults who have screwed up everything in the first place. Why do they get to make the decisions when they've done such stupid things?'

'Yeah, I know.'

'Children are the weakest minority.'

'Only eighteen months to eighteen.'

She tried to smile. 'Twenty for me.'

'We'll get through this.'

She glanced at the field. In the distance, some people

were kicking around a football. The school's red-and-white façade seemed so far away. Everything looked as though she was gazing at it through the soft focus lens of melancholy. No filter, of course.

'Add another to the Split club, huh?' she said, and squeezed his hand. 'We've *got* to get through this.'

Somehow she had a feeling they would. *Somehow.*

'Did you know there are 1442 kilometres between Delhi and Bombay?' said Noor to Sanvi on the phone that evening.

'That's not a lot,' said Sanvi, yawning.

'Oh, I'm *sorry,* am I *boring* you with my heart's woes?'

'Don't be an ass,' said Sanvi. 'I've joined an early-morning cycling group with some friends. We went for a ride today at 5 a.m. before school. I'm *exhausted.*'

'5 a.m.! You're nuts.'

'I feel a bit nuts. But it's lots of fun. It's not just us, it's also some other grown-ups but they're also cool.'

'Maybe I'll join you one day,' said Noor. 'After all, I'll need to keep myself occupied when Ishaan is *one thousand four hundred and forty two* kilometres away.'

'Oh relax,' said Sanvi, yawning again. 'Aryan is going to spend the summer in Goa with some friends, so you and I will go visit your grandparents and then we'll take Ishaan and go to Goa as well.'

'Oh, that sounds lovely! But I can't see *any* of our adults agreeing to this plan.'

'Leave that to me, darling.' And Noor knew she could.

If there was ever anyone who could devise a way to get to Goa without people knowing *why* or *with whom* she was going, it was Sanvi. Noor had a faint flash of prophecy just then: Sanvi would emerge from her teens as a mysterious adult, a person who always had 'plans' but you wouldn't know what they were until they happened.

Just then, there was a knock on the door and Noor looked up and Natasha walked in.

'Sanvi, I've got to go, Natasha just came in the door. Yes, *Natasha*. No, we didn't have plans. Okay, I'll talk to you tomorrow.'

It was strange to see Natasha just standing at the doorway like that, her hands dangling loosely by her side. She hadn't brought her music, none that Noor could see, so she looked inexplicably naked, no giant headphones around her neck. Noor flashbacked to when Natasha had been here last—so long ago, before Ammi left—and how they had almost fallen over laughing at something that she couldn't remember now. They used to laugh a lot together, Noor had always thought that was one of the things that *made* their friendship. She didn't laugh that much in the company of anyone else, not Ishaan, not Sanvi.

'Hey,' said Natasha, still standing awkwardly.

'Hey!' said Noor, and gestured to her to come in. Natasha perched herself on the edge of the bed.

'I told my parents to drop me off here—they were on their way out. I hope you don't mind.'

'Nope.'

'It's sort of *quiet* here without your mum, isn't it?' Then, making a face to apologize, 'I'm sorry, I just meant . . .'

'It's cool, I know what you meant.'

'Listen, Noor,' Natasha gazed at Noor's Zayn collage for a bit, trying to summon up courage. 'I'm really sorry for the way I acted. You know, sort of zoning out on you and all. I didn't know you had so much shit going on in your life or I never would have.'

So here it was at last. The Natasha apology. Strangely, Noor didn't feel any different now that it was all out in the open. She realized she just didn't care that much. It was an interesting feeling. An *adult* feeling.

'It's fine,' she said. 'But *why* did you? Just out of curiosity?'

'I don't know. I mean, I wanted to be with Prateek and you were being kind of strange about it, so I decided to hang with Armana for a while.'

'*She* was being weird too!'

'Yeah, I know, but with her it was okay because it was expected. But with you, I don't know, I sort of wanted you to know how I felt without telling you about it. I know it's unfair.'

'I get it, I think.'

'Armana's nice, but she's not *nice*, you know?'

Noor smiled. She *did* know.

'How's it going with Prateek anyway?'

'Eh,' Natasha waved a hand dismissively in the air. 'It's over, I think. He's not all *that*.'

So Natasha's romance was over. She was sort of fickle for all that. Both with boys and with friendships. But still, she was the only person who used to be able to make Noor laugh till she gasped for breath.

That was then, Noor thought. The old Noor. The-before-Ammi-left Noor. The-before Ishaan-loved-me Noor. This Noor examined Natasha as she got comfortable and wondered if their friendship would ever be the same again. *Oh well. Time will tell.*

And then she caught up with Natasha about all the things they had been doing in the weeks they hadn't seen each other properly.

Text message 1, Noor to Ishaan
Hey. You awake?

Text message 2, Ishaan to Noor
Yeah. Just watching some TV, thinking of you. ;)

Text message 3, Noor to Ishaan
I was wrong, btw.

Text message 4, Ishaan to Noor
About what?

Text message 5, Noor to Ishaan
Ok, here goes: I DO love you. I love you. I was stupid to not say so before. I love you very very very much.

Text message 6, Ishaan to Noor
You make me so happy.

Text message 7, Ishaan to Noor
I love you too, by the way, in case you were wondering why I hadn't said it back. I was just so blown away.

Text message 8, Noor to Ishaan
I wasn't wondering. ☺

Text message 9, Ishaan to Noor
Will we rent a flat in Bombay together one day?

Text message 10, Noor to Ishaan
20 months

Text message 11, Ishaan to Noor
I can't wait.

Text message 12, Noor to Ishaan
☺

Text message 13, Ishaan to Noor
☺

Dear Ammi,

I'm not angry with you anymore. I WAS. I was super angry. But then I had time to get used to the idea, and I get why you did it. I don't think it was cool of you to leave me and 'US' without any warning and if you could do it again, would you do it differently?

Everything is fine here. Dad and I are managing. Daadi is leaving next week to go back to Jaipur. We didn't exactly get along but she made it a little bit easier. Now it's going to be just me and Dad. That'll be weird but we're talking more now. I'm thinking of asking him to get me a dog. (Unless you think you're going to come back. ARE you? I know you're allergic to dogs. Although, I don't know if it would work if you moved back now. Too much has happened.)

I don't know what Sunny Uncle is like, or why you think he's better for you than Dad. Dad's fantastic, I think.

I have a boyfriend now. He was in this divorce club at school that Saras Ma'am said you made me join. I guess it was a good idea after all. He's moving back to Bombay soon, though. I'm not sure I'll go back to the club after he leaves, but I might see Saras Ma'am once a week, just to talk about things.

It's good to have people to talk to.

Do you love Sunny Uncle? Do you love him more than you love Dad? LOVED, I mean.

I think I'd like to see you once you get back to Delhi. Not HIM. I'm not ready to meet HIM. But you and I need to talk, I think.

I miss you, Ammi. I might still be a little mad. But I miss you anyway.

Love,

Noorie

ACKNOWLEDGEMENTS

This book would not be here at all if it weren't for the awesomeness of Ameya Nagarajan, brilliant friend and brilliant-er editor, and I know the old trope of 'not working with your friends' but it actually totally worked for us, so yay! Girl power! Ameya, take a bow!

Thanks also to Nayantara Sood, Supriya Sodhi, Meghna Mehta Hazarika, Samyukta Bhowmick, Samit Basu and my own particular set of ladies I've grown old with, who are all much nicer than the Group in this book: Isheeta Gupta, Neha Kaul Mehra, Prerna Chawla and Nayantara Rai.

I have so many other people in my life that I am lucky, lucky, LUCKY for, and you may think this is a cop-out, just calling you 'one of those people' but thank you for being so supportive and amazing anyway. I'm leaving this line especially blank so I can fill your name in when I see you:

My dad, who passed on a scientific mind and a love for books and writing: I'll always be grateful for those two things!

And finally, the love of my life and my partner in crime: Kian Ganz, who is not unlike Ishaan, since he's absolutely dreamy. (**doodles hearts around his name**)